The Adventures of
Parsley the Lion

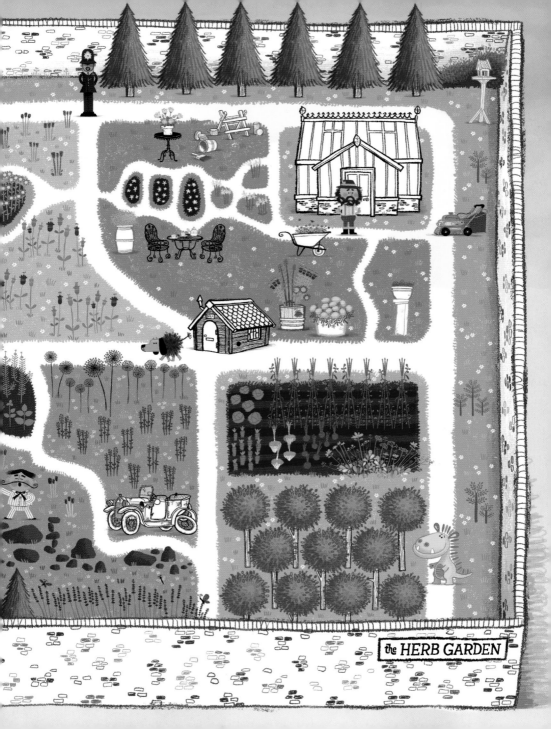

the HERB GARDEN

For Sharon and Peter
– R. B.

This edition first published in hardback in Great Britain by
HarperCollins *Children's Books* in 2020

Part 1 first published as *Parsley the Lion* in Great Britain
in Young Lions by William Collins Sons and Co. Ltd in 1972
Part 2 first published as *Parsley Parade* in Great Britain
in Armada Lions by William Collins Sons and Co. Ltd in 1972

William Collins Sons and Co. Ltd and HarperCollins *Children's Books*
are divisions of HarperCollins*Publishers* Ltd,
HarperCollins Publishers
1 London Bridge Street
London SE1 9GF

The HarperCollins website address is
www.harpercollins.co.uk

1

Text copyright © Michael Bond 1972, 2020
Illustrations copyright © Rob Biddulph 2020
All rights reserved

LIMITED EDITION ISBN: 978-0-00-844489-1
HB ISBN: 978-0-00-798297-4

Michael Bond and Rob Biddulph assert the moral right to be identified as the author and illustrator of the work respectively.
A CIP catalogue record for this title is available from the British Library.

Typeset in Bitstream Cooper BT 11/20pt
Printed and bound in England by CPI Group (UK) Ltd, Croydon CR0 4YY
A CIP catalogue record for this title is available from the British Library.

MIX
Paper from
responsible sources
FSC™ C007454

FSC
www.fsc.org

This book is produced from independently certified FSC™ paper to ensure responsible forest management.

Find out more about HarperCollins and the environment at www.harpercollins.co.uk/green

MICHAEL BOND

The Adventures of

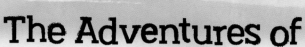

ParSLey the Lion

Illustrated by *Rob Biddulph*

HarperCollins *Children's Books*

PARSLEY

SAGE

DILL

MR BAYLEAF

MR ONION AND THE CHIVES

CONSTABLE KNAPWEED

SIR BASIL

LADY ROSEMARY

SIGNOR SOLIDAGO

MRS ONION

PASHANA BEDHI

TARRAGON

AUNT MINT

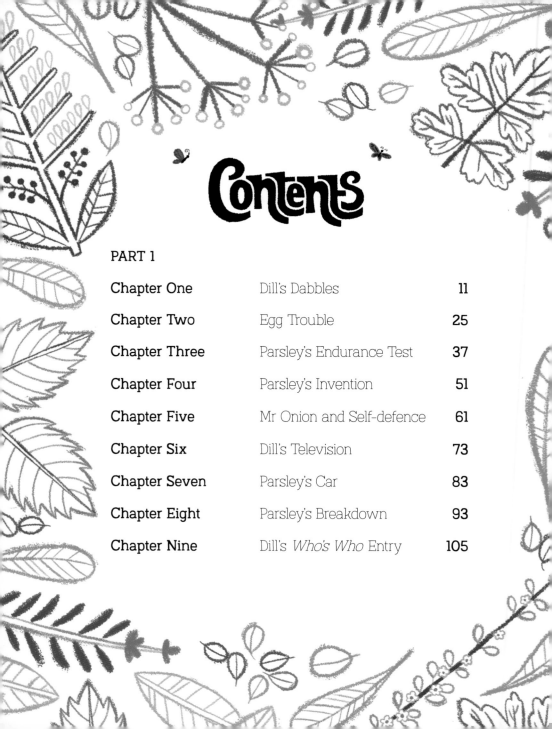

Contents

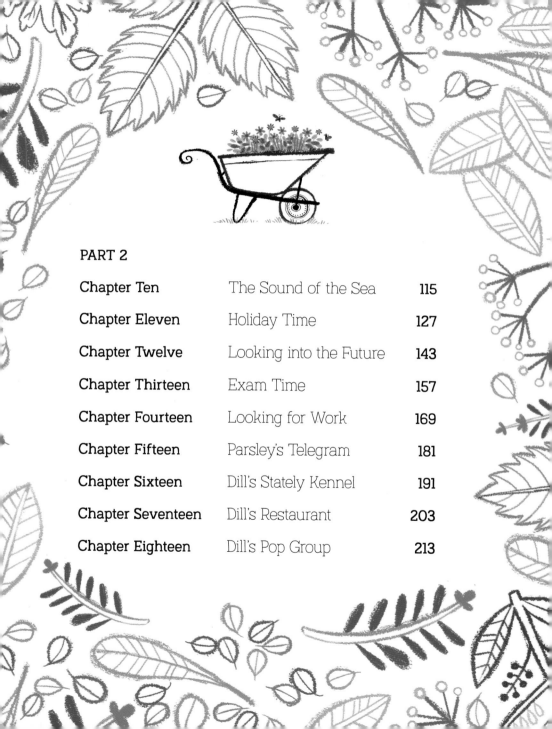

PART 2

PART 1

Chapter 1

DILL'S DABBLES

One of the nicest things about being a lion called Parsley and living in the Herb Garden is that he is never, ever quite sure what's going to happen to him next.

The only thing he is completely sure about is the fact that when it does happen his friend, Dill the dog, won't be far away.

Dill is the kind of dog who always has some surprise or other up his paw; and if it isn't up his paw it's just as likely to be hanging from the nearest bush.

For instance, there was the time he held his 'dabbles' exhibition.

Being fond of an early morning stroll, Parsley was first on the scene and he stopped in his tracks, hardly able to believe his eyes, as he peered along the path leading between Dill's kennel and Mr Bayleaf's greenhouse.

Lining the banks on either side, and stretching away into the distance as far as the eye could see, were pieces of cardboard. There were square pieces, tall pieces, long pieces; some with squiggles on them, some without. There were large ones, small ones, blank ones and black ones. Parsley had never seen anything quite like it before and he blinked several times in order to make sure he wasn't dreaming.

'It's either been raining cardboard,' he said, addressing the world in general, 'or else Mr Bayleaf's had a nasty accident with his

14

2o

dustbin.' And he was about to set to work clearing things up
when a familiar, if slightly muffled, voice made him stop in
his tracks.

Parsley looked round and then did a large double-take. The
voice was Dill's. The size and shape of the owner of the voice
was definitely Dill-like – short, round, furry and doglike. But
there the resemblance ended, for if there was any fur it was
safely hidden beneath an enormous brightly coloured smock,
and the head – or what little could be seen of it – was encased in
a large black beret, which flopped down on either side over both
ears, and beneath which hung a loosely knotted cravat.

'How do you like my ensemble?' enquired Dill.

'I don't know about your ensemble,' replied Parsley. 'I'm more worried about the way you're dressed. What's going on? And what are all these bits of cardboard everywhere?'

'Bits of cardboard?' repeated Dill stiffly. '*Bits of cardboard?* I'll have you know these "bits of cardboard", as you call them, happen to be works of art!'

Parsley stared at Dill as if he could hardly believe his ears – which he couldn't. 'Works of art?' he exclaimed. 'You don't mean to say you've taken up painting?'

Dill lowered his gaze modestly. 'I dabble a bit,' he said carelessly. 'I'm holding a one-dog exhibition of some of my best dabbles at the moment. It's in aid of National Dog Bone Week.'

'It looks more like National Rubbish Week to me,' said Parsley. He peered at a piece of plain white cardboard hanging from a nearby bush. 'What's that meant to be, for goodness' sake?'

Dill followed his gaze and then consulted a large catalogue on the ground by his paws. 'Number thirty-one,' he said, riffling through the pages. 'I've called it *White Cat in a Snowstorm*. Do you like it?'

'Do I like it?' repeated Parsley doubtfully. 'Er . . . well, yes . . . and then again . . . no.'

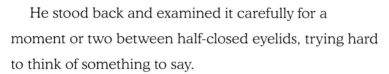

He stood back and examined it carefully for a moment or two between half-closed eyelids, trying hard to think of something to say.

'It has length . . . and breadth . . . and, er . . .'

'It's for sale,' broke in Dill hopefully.

'In that case,' said Parsley hastily, 'I definitely don't like it.'

Dill's face dropped. 'I *was* hoping I might be able to put you down for a dozen or so,' he announced.

'A dozen or so?' repeated Parsley in alarm. 'I have a job finding room for Christmas cards in my den, let alone paintings.'

'Well, perhaps a couple, then,' said Dill. He nodded towards a piece of black card hanging from a bush on the opposite side of the track. 'That one's called *Black Cat in a Coal Cellar*. I can let you have the two as a matching pair for the price of one if you like.'

'I can let you have a hollow laugh for nothing,' said Parsley.

'You wait,' exclaimed Dill. 'They used to laugh at Picasso. Give it a while and these'll be selling like hot cakes.'

'Hot cakes, maybe,' began Parsley. 'But paintings . . . never!'

'Shh!' Dill put a paw to his lips as he caught the sound of footsteps coming along the path. 'This could be a buyer. Let's hide and see what happens.'

'That's not a buyer,' said Parsley as a wheelbarrow came into view. He peered through a gap in the shrubbery. 'That's Bayleaf!'

Sir Basil's gardener seemed to be reacting to Dill's exhibition in much the same way as Parsley had.

He took off his hat and stood for a moment or two scratching his head in disbelief as he took in the scene. Then he went up to the nearest painting and examined it more closely. After that he stood back and began viewing it from all angles, first with his head to one side, then with it on the other. Then he took a tape measure from his pocket and held it up to the frame.

'Arrh!' he said at last. 'Oooh, arrrh! Arrrh, that's fine, that is. That be just what I need to 'ang in my greenhouse.'

Dill nudged Parsley triumphantly. 'There you are!' he cried. 'What did I tell you?'

'Wonders will never cease,' murmured Parsley.

'I reckon,' continued Bayleaf to himself, 'I reckon that'd be just the right size for bunging up that there 'ole behind my begonias. Keep the draught out a treat that would.'

'Ahem,' said Parsley as Bayleaf picked up his barrow and went on his way. 'So much for art.'

'Typical!' snorted Dill in disgust.

'No soul – that's Bayleaf's trouble. No appreciation of the finer things in life.'

Parsley turned his attention to another painting further along the row and standing a little apart from the rest. It was large and brown and smeary.

'I should think your trouble's lack of paint,' he exclaimed, sniffing the canvas. 'What's all this stuff?'

'Ah, that was something I did during my gravy period,' said Dill vaguely. 'I knocked a jug over by mistake one Sunday lunchtime and when I licked it up that's what happened!'

Parsley took a closer look at the work in question and then shuddered. 'It figures,' he said, hurrying on to the next painting. 'And what's this one?'

'Ah,' said Dill dreamily. 'Now you really need to stand back to appreciate that one. That's my masterpiece. Who does it remind you of?'

Parsley considered the matter for a moment or two.

'If I said the word "Monet" to you,' prompted Dill, mentioning the first famous painter he could think of, 'what would you say?'

'I'd say your pronunciation wasn't very good,' said Parsley. 'The word I was thinking of was *monstrous*. How *can* you?'

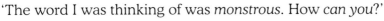

'Oh, it's quite easy really,' panted Dill, running round and round in circles. 'I get some bones and boil them all up to make the gravy. Then I pour it over the canvas, and then . . .'

'I know,' shuddered Parsley. 'You lick it up . . .'

'You may scoff,' said Dill, 'but it must be nice to leave something behind when you go. I'd like to think that people will remember me long after the time comes for the big Vet on high to call me to the kennel in the sky.'

Parsley cast his eye along the row of paintings. 'If you leave things like that behind,' he said, 'I should think your wish will be granted. They'll never forget you.'

'Ahem,' said Dill, giving his friend a nudge, 'I don't wish to say "I told you so", but you must admit I did tell you so.' He lowered his voice. 'Look over your shoulder. This could be my big breakthrough.'

Parsley followed the direction of Dill's gaze towards a small group at the far end of the path. It was made up of Sir Basil, Lady Rosemary and Constable Knapweed, and they were peering hard at a large and rather evil-looking head-and-shoulders portrait, which appeared to be hung in a place of honour.

Constable Knapweed in particular seemed most impressed by it and he was holding forth at great length to the others.

His voice floated along the path. 'Now this is what I call a good picture,' he announced. 'When I 'eard what was going on I did 'ave 'alf a mind to speak to young Dill about it, but I take it all back now.'

Dill's cravat began to tremble with excitement. 'You see,' he hissed. 'What did I tell you? Fame at last!'

Lady Rosemary examined the picture carefully through her lorgnette. 'It's certainly most unusual,' she agreed. '*Most* unusual.'

'Reminds me of someone,' said Sir Basil. 'Can't think who.'

'Whoever it is,' said Constable Knapweed, 'young Dill's really captured the full villainy of the person behind the face. Got under the skin as you might say. Look at those shifty eyes. And that chin. He's a nasty piece of work, all right. I wouldn't touch 'im with a barge pole – not unless it was in the line of duty as you might say. Shows you the sort of character we in the force are up against. I'd like to buy that and 'ave some copies made so as I could 'ang them up on all the trees in the Herb Garden to act as a warning.'

'Jolly good idea,' interrupted Sir Basil. 'What's it called, Rosemary?'

Lady Rosemary ran her eyes down the catalogue. 'Number twenty-four,' she said. '*Portrait of Constable Knapweed*.'

'What's that?' bellowed Constable Knapweed, his eyes nearly popping out of his head. 'A portrait of *me*?'

As if by magic his notebook appeared in one hand, his pencil in the other.

'Where is he? I'll throw the book at him! . . . I'll 'ave him for painting without a licence! . . . I'll 'ave him for leaving litter about unattended! I'll . . .'

'I have a feeling,' began Parsley, 'that Constable Knapweed wants you for something!' But Dill had already disappeared behind the nearest bush.

'Do you want to buy a
genuine Constable painting?'
he called. 'I know where there's one going cheap.
It hasn't even been to the cleaner's yet. The paint's still wet.'

Constable Knapweed tapped Parsley on his mane. 'Where is
he? Which way did he go?' he demanded.

Parsley did an imitation of Dill and turned round and round
several times quickly before replying. 'Er . . . I'm not quite sure,'
he answered truthfully, for by then he was feeling so giddy one
bush looked very like another. He looked to his right. 'It may
have been that way. On the other hand –' he looked to his left –
'it may have been that way.'

'Well, whichever way it was,' growled Constable Knapweed,
'I'll 'ave him. Make no mistake. I'll 'ave him before the day's out.'

As Constable Knapweed hurried on his way the leaves on a
nearby bush parted and Dill poked his head out. 'Has he gone?'
he asked. 'I say, do you think you could put me up in your den
for a day or two? Just until all the fuss dies down. I'll paint your
portrait for nothing if you'll let me.'

Parsley looked at him disbelievingly. 'Let *you* paint *my*
portrait?' he exclaimed. 'After all that's

happened? You must be joking.'

'Don't move,' called Dill as Parsley made to leave. 'Stay exactly as you are.'

Parsley paused, interested in spite of himself. 'Why?' he demanded.

'Oh, nothing really,' said Dill. 'It's just that it's difficult finding faces of real character these days. That firm jaw . . . that forehead . . . those cheekbones . . . The light was catching you in a certain way and for a moment I thought perhaps . . . but never mind . . .'

Parsley looked round at all the paintings and then gave a deep sigh. Somehow, with Dill, even when he knew he was letting himself in for something he still managed to let himself in for it, despite all the warning voices.

'Come on,' he called. 'What are we waiting for?'

Dill needed no second bidding. 'I'll just get my brushes and my palette and my easel,' he called as he rushed on ahead. 'And while I'm doing all that . . .'

'I know,' said Parsley resignedly. 'I'll put the gravy on to boil!'

Chapter 2

EGG TROUBLE

One morning, soon after Dill's painting exhibition, Parsley was having a quiet doze in the Herb Garden when he was wakened by a loud thud.

When he opened his eyes he found a small, round object by his side.

'That's very strange,' he said, looking up at the sky. 'There was nothing in the weather forecast this morning about gale-force eggs!'

In the end he decided to go and see his friend Dill about the matter and, picking the egg up carefully in his mouth, he made his way towards Dill's kennel.

'Knock! Knock!' he called as he stood outside the door.

'Who's there?' came an answering voice.

'It's me,' said Parsley.

The door opened and Dill stood there rubbing his eyes.

'I'm sorry to wake you,' said Parsley.

'That's all right,' said Dill. 'I had to get up anyway. There was somebody at the door. What's the trouble?'

Parsley laid the egg on Dill's doorstep. 'That!' he said simply. 'What have you got to say about *that*?'

Dill peered at the object from several angles.

'Yums,' he said at last.

'Is that all?' asked Parsley.

'Well,' said Dill, 'I mean, it's obviously an egg of some kind. And once you've seen one you've seen the lot. I mean, what *can* you say about an egg?'

'I *was* hoping for something better than "yums",' said Parsley.

'All right, then,' said Dill. He took a deep breath and put on his best reciting voice. 'Eggs come in many sizes and colours. They can be fried, boiled, poached, scrambled, dropped—'

'And they can be *thrown*,' broke in Parsley meaningly. 'Thanks for your help. I don't know what I would have done without it.'

'You're welcome,' said Dill as he closed his door. 'Give me a shout when it's cooked,' he called. 'I'll come and help you eat it.'

'Dogs!' exclaimed Parsley, addressing the letter box. 'I shall take my problem elsewhere.'

So he took it to Aunt Mint.

Aunt Mint laid down her knitting and peered at the object through her glasses.

'What a strange-looking egg,' she said. 'I don't think I've ever seen a perfectly *round* egg before. I shall knit it a cosy.

That's what I shall do. Knit it a nice, round cosy.'

Parsley's next visit was to Pashana Bedhi, the chef who lived at the back of the Herb Garden and who knew about most things.

Pashana Bedhi was standing by the path stirring his lunch with a long silver spoon when Parsley arrived.

Taking the spoon out of the pot, he tried tapping it on the egg, but it seemed to do more harm to the spoon than the egg.

'Oh dear,' he said, 'this is a very *hard* egg. A very *hard* egg indeed. In all my years of cooking I have never come across anything as *hard* as this egg. If you are trying to crack this egg, I should be very careful of your spoon, otherwise it may end up like mine!'

Next Parsley tried Mr Onion.

Mr Onion was the schoolmaster and Parsley felt sure he would know all there was to know about eggs, but as it turned out Mr

Onion was no more help than
the others.

'This egg,' he said, holding it up to the light, 'is round and
covered all over with small spots. It is obviously the egg of the
lesser-spotted whatjemecallit. A bird noted for the fact that it lays
round eggs . . . er . . . covered all over with small spots.'

'Isn't it amazing,' said Parsley as Mr Onion went on his way.
'You'd think if people didn't know the answer to something
they'd say so.

'I mean –' he took a closer look at the object – 'anyone can
see it's an egg and it's got spots.'

He placed it on the ground and tried jumping on it. 'Ow! And
you only have to jump on it to see that it's hard.'

Parsley tried looking for Constable Knapweed, but he was
out on his rounds; and Mr Bayleaf, the gardener, was much too

busy with his vegetable patch to bother about such trifling matters as eggs. Even Sir Basil and Lady Rosemary were nowhere to be seen, so Parsley decided to do what he knew he ought to have done in the first place – consult his book.

Parsley had the most marvellous book. Within its covers it had everything about everything, and he was soon flipping through the pages. Past A for 'orses,* through the Bs and Cs and the Ds . . . past G for goodness' sake** and – at last – back a page or two, he peered at the entry under E for eggs.

'If you want to find out more about an egg,' it said, 'why not try hatching it and see what comes out!'

'What a masterly plan!' exclaimed Parsley, gazing at the page in admiration.

'I suppose I could try sitting on it . . .' He lowered himself gently on to the egg. It was very uncomfortable. 'On the other hand . . .' He gazed upwards and as he did so a slow smile came over his face. 'On the other hand, it's really much more of a job for an owl.'

'What's that?' called Sage the owl as he hopped down beside Parsley. 'What did you tu whit, tu say?'

Parsley pointed to the object at his feet. 'I was about to say,'

* Sounds like 'hay for horses' – part of a joke alphabet
** Sounds like 'gee, for goodness' sake'

he continued, 'that you have been selected from thousands of applicants for the honour of hatching this most unusual egg.'

'Tu whit, tu whoooo!' hooted Sage excitedly. 'How many applicants did you say?'

'Well, er . . . two or three . . .' said Parsley.

'Tu whit, *tu* or *three*,' hooted Sage disappointedly.

'Look,' said Parsley impatiently, 'you're the only bird we've got. If you're going to be difficult . . . Besides, one egg's not going to hurt you . . .'

'I shouldn't speak too soon,' said Dill, hurrying on to the scene. 'Look!' And he laid a second egg alongside the first one. 'And there are plenty more where this one came from. Come and have a look.'

'Two eggs?' hooted Sage. 'Tu whit, *tu* whoo eggs?'

Parsley gazed after Dill, who had just disappeared behind a bush. 'Er, I have to go and see a dog about some eggs,' he said. 'I shan't be long . . .'

'Here you are,' said Dill when Parsley joined him. He nodded towards a small pile of eggs he'd collected, all exactly the same as each other. 'What did I tell you?'

'Good gracious!' exclaimed Parsley. 'They either belong to a very tall bird or it's been raining eggs. That's six!'

'Fore!' said a voice from behind him.

'Six,' said Parsley. 'There are four here and I had two. Four and two is six.'

'I didn't say anything!' exclaimed Dill. 'Don't grumble at me.'

As he spoke there was a plop and yet another 'egg' landed on the ground beside them.

'Heavens above!' cried Parsley. 'That makes seven!'

'Fore!' said the voice behind him again.

'Look,' said Parsley impatiently. 'You've got *four* on the brain. It's about time you went back to school. Five and two is seven.'

'I haven't even opened my mouth,' wailed Dill.

'Well, someone did,' said Parsley.

'Either that,' said Dill, nearly jumping out of his skin as there was another plop just behind him, 'or it's a ghost. I'm getting out of here. What with eggs and voices . . .'

'Shh!' said Parsley. 'Listen. Talking of voices, that sounds like Lady Rosemary.'

Dill fell silent as Lady Rosemary's voice floated across the shrubbery.

'Sage!' she cried. 'You naughty owl! What *are* you doin'? Sittin' on Sir Basil's golf balls. He's been lookin' for them everywhere. Really! What will you be up to next?'

'Golf balls?' hooted Sage. 'I've been trying tu whit, tu hatch *golf balls*?' Sage sounded more than a trifle annoyed.

Parsley and Dill exchanged glances. 'No wonder they felt hard,' murmured Parsley.

'Suppose one had landed on our heads,' said Dill.

'The mind boggles!' agreed Parsley.

'Fore!'* came a voice, closer at hand this time, and clearly recognisable as belonging to Sir Basil.

'Watch out!' cried Dill. 'Sir Basil's at it again!'

* Golfers shout 'Fore!' to warn others of flying golf balls.

'Come on,' said Parsley. 'I'm going!'

There was a plop beside them.

'Sure you won't have another?' asked Dill.

'No, thank you,' said Parsley. 'I'm trying to give them up! Once you've seen one you've seen the lot.'

❊Chapter 3

PARSLEY'S ENDURANCE TEST

There's only one thing Parsley likes better than an hour's nap after lunch, and that's a two-hour's nap.

The only trouble is the Herb Garden isn't always as peaceful as it might be.

For instance, if there's one thing Mr Bayleaf, the gardener, likes better than an hour's nap after lunch it's cutting Sir Basil's lawn with his lawnmower.

Give him a shower of rain followed by some sunshine to make the grass grow and he's away.

And if it isn't the sound of lawnmowers it's police whistles. If Constable Knapweed caught a criminal every time he blew his whistle there would be nowhere to put them all.

On the other hand, even that isn't as bad as the days when Mr Onion gives the Chives singing lessons.

They only know one song and Parsley's heard it so many times he can sing it backwards – and often does when he's trying to get to sleep!

It goes:

Because we are so many Chives,
And dressed like one another,
It makes it even hard to tell,
A sister from a brother.

But the worst time of all is when Sage is in one of his chirpy moods. It doesn't happen often, but when it does, no one, least of all Parsley, stands a chance of getting any sleep.

Sage's chirp is a cross between a circular saw, a rusty mangle and a door badly in need of a spot of oil on its hinges.

It was on just such a day – a day when Bayleaf took it into his head to cut the grass, Constable Knapweed was at his most officious, the Chives' voices had never been louder or shriller and Sage's chirps never so ghastly – that Parsley decided to see what his friend Dill had to say on the matter.

He hurried along the path through the Herb Garden and had nearly reached Dill's kennel when he trod on something sharp.

In fact, not just something, but lots of things.

'Oh!' he cried. 'Oooh! Ow! Oooooh!'

Dill appeared at his front door. 'What's up?' he called.

'Anything the matter? I was in the middle of a good after-lunch nap. You woke me up!'

'*I* woke *you* up!' snorted Parsley, hopping from one paw to the other. 'I've just trodden on something sharp!'

'I expect it was my tin-tacks,' said Dill carelessly. 'I sometimes put them down to keep away the wolves.'

'Wolves?' Parsley forgot about the pain in his paws and stared at his friend. 'But there aren't any wolves in the Herb Garden.'

'There you are,' said Dill. 'That shows how well they work.'

'It's no good!' groaned Parsley. 'I shall either have to join the Noise Abatement Society or consult my book, and as I haven't got any application forms to join the Noise Abatement Society on me I think I'd better consult my book.'

Leaving Dill to go back to sleep, Parsley returned to his den and was soon riffling through the pages of his book. Through the 'needles' and on past 'noddles' until he came to the section headed 'noises'.

'"Noises",' he read, '"are often caused by lawnmowers, constables blowing whistles, Chives singing and owls chirping."'

He looked up. 'It's absolutely right, you know,' he exclaimed. 'It couldn't be more right.

'"These noises",' he read on, '"often happen because the people who make them have nothing better to do. Why not try giving them an *endurance test!*"'

Parsley looked up again. *I suppose it's worth a go*, he thought. Or rather he tried to think, above the sound of the lawnmower, the whistles, the singing and the chirps. *In fact*, he thought, anything's *better than this!*

For the next half hour or so Parsley was extremely busy with some paper, a pen and a ruler, and shortly after he had finished the rest of the Herb Garden was brought to life by the sound of the school bell.

Apart from early in the morning when Mr Onion called the Chives to their lessons, it was very rare for the school bell to be rung and everyone knew it must be something very important.

'Oyez! Oyez!' called Parsley as he pulled on the rope. 'Hear ye! Hear ye!

'Get your entry forms here for the Grand Endurance Test.

'There will be a prize for whosoever does whatsoever for longer than ever.

'Oyez! Oyez!'

Bayleaf picked up a form from the pile by Parsley's side.

'An endurance test?' he said. 'Oh, arrh. I got just the idea for that I 'ave.' And he hurried off as fast as his legs would carry him.

A moment later his lawnmower burst into life and less than a moment after that he came shooting into view again.

'I'm going to see how far I can go afore I'm worn out,' he called as he shot past. 'I be going to endure going farther and faster than anyone ever 'as afore.

Darned if I don't reach Australia afore I've finished.'

43

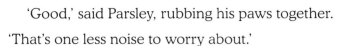

'Good,' said Parsley, rubbing his paws together. 'That's one less noise to worry about.'

'An endurance test?' said Constable Knapweed, copying the particulars from the form into his notebook. 'Whosoever does whatsoever for longer than ever. Well, now . . . that's easy. There's no problem there.'

Undoing the top pocket of his uniform, he withdrew a whistle and began to blow.

'Peeeeeeeep!' he went. 'Peeeeeeeeeep! Peeeeeeeeeeeeep!'

'I shall blow my whistle,' he announced. 'Peeeeeeeeep . . . longer . . . peeeeeeeeeep . . . and harder . . . peeeeeeeeeep . . . and more often than anyone ever has before.'

And to show that he meant business he gave his whistle such a hard blow his cheeks puffed out over the strap of his helmet.

But the noise that came out nowhere matched the effort that went into it.

In fact, as whistles go, it was definitely a non-starter, like the gurgling sound that might be made by the waste pipe on a very tiny washbasin.

Constable Knapweed took the whistle from his mouth and

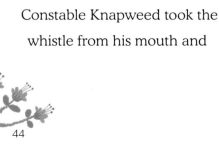

examined it carefully. 'My pea's gone soggy!' he exclaimed at last. 'That's what's happened. My pea's gone soggy!'

'Marvellous,' said Parsley. 'Couldn't be better. I'll have it with some chips for dinner tonight. Soggy pea and chips. Nothing nicer!'

Constable Knapweed was about to hold forth on the subject of whistles, peas and lions in general – not to mention Parsley in particular – when the sound of marching feet heralded the arrival of the Chives and Mr Onion.

Mr Onion brought his platoon to a halt in front of Parsley.

'Now, Chives,' he shouted, 'as you all know we are about to enter for the Grand Endurance Test.

'This endurance test will take the form of singing while on the march. The Chive who can march the furthest and sing the loudest will be the winner and will receive the Grand award. Chiiiives, marching and singing, by numbers, begin . . . Left . . . left . . . left, right, left.'

And the Chives all burst into song.

'Because we are so many Chives,
And dressed like one another,
It makes it even hard to tell,
A sister from a brother.'

'Phantasmagorical!' said Parsley as the sound of their voices died away into the bushes. 'That's the only word for it.'

'An endurance test?' hooted Sage the owl, jumping down from his nest. 'Tu whit, tu whoo. There's no one who can tu whit, tu whistle louder and longer than I can!'

And to show the truth of what he was saying Sage let fly with a shrill whistle. He puffed out his cheeks and he lifted his beak

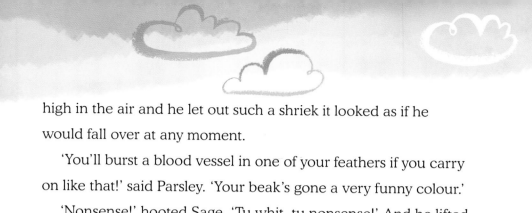

high in the air and he let out such a shriek it looked as if he
would fall over at any moment.

'You'll burst a blood vessel in one of your feathers if you carry
on like that!' said Parsley. 'Your beak's gone a very funny colour.'

'Nonsense!' hooted Sage. 'Tu whit, tu nonsense!' And he lifted
up his head and had a second go.

'That,' said Parsley as Sage's whistle died away in much the
same way as Constable Knapweed's had, 'is what happens to
owls who whistle tu whit, tu much!'

'What am I going to do?' hooted Sage.

'What am I going tu whit, tu do now?'

'I should take a trip down to the nearest pet shop,' said Parsley. 'You often find birds going cheep there. You might be able to buy one and borrow his whistle.'

As Sage hopped on his way Parsley settled down and closed his eyes.

How very peaceful it seemed. No lawnmowers. No whistles being blown. No singing. No owls cheeping. Not a sound to disturb the peace . . . except . . .

From somewhere close at hand there was a low rumbling. At least, it was a noise that started off as a low rumble but seemed to end as a kind of sizzling sound.

Parsley sat up and consulted his book.

'"Low rumbling noises with sizzles at the end",' it said, '"are usually caused by dogs going in for snoring endurance tests."'

And once again Parsley's book was all too right. As he drew nearer and nearer to

Dill's kennel the snores grew louder and louder.

'Have you come to give me my prize?' asked Dill when Parsley shook him awake.

'No, I haven't,' growled Parsley.

Dill smacked his lips. 'I'm quietly confident,' he said.

'It doesn't sound very quiet to me,' replied Parsley.

'I've been doing it for five minutes already,' broke in Dill. 'Do you think I shall win first prize?'

'No,' said Parsley. 'I don't. But move over . . . you've got some pretty stiff competition coming up. If you ask me my endurance has been tested as much as anyone's today.' He gave a large yawn. 'I'm so tired now I could endure anything. Even your snores. Goodnight!'

⸙Chapter 4

PARSLEY'S INVENTION

One morning Parsley woke with a strange feeling that he would like to invent something.

'I feel very inventive today,' he announced to the world in general.

The only trouble was he couldn't think of a single thing that hadn't been thought of before. Nails with threads on them so that they could be screwed into wood; windows with glass in them to keep out the rain; everything, but everything, seemed to have been invented already.

'How about an everlasting bone?' asked Dill when Parsley mentioned the matter to him.

Parsley shook his head. 'You wouldn't like it,' he said. 'You'd soon get fed up.'

'Try me and see,' cried Dill, running round and round in a circle. 'You just try me and see.'

'Perhaps I could invent the wheel,' said Parsley dreamily. 'Think of all the things you could do with a wheel.'

'It's been done,' said Dill gloomily. 'Bayleaf's had one on his wheelbarrow for years.'

'You can't trust anyone these days,' said Parsley. 'There must be *something*.'

Dill sat down and pondered the matter for a moment or two. 'How about a windmill for grinding smoke?' he suggested.

'A windmill for grinding smoke?' repeated Parsley. 'That may be all right for the export trade, but how about the home market? How many windmills do you see when you're out for a walk?'

'Well,' said Dill, 'how about a machine for squeezing toothpaste back into the tube, then? I'm always squeezing too much out of mine and I can never get it back in.'

'Look,' said Parsley impatiently, 'if you can't think of anything sensible to invent . . .'

'In that case,' said Dill, 'it's back to everlasting bones. You can't have anything more sensible than that.'

Parsley glared at him. 'Did Stephenson have all this trouble when he invented rockets?' he asked.

'I don't expect so,' said Dill.

'Did Sir Isaac Newton have all this trouble when he invented the apple?' asked Parsley.

'I shouldn't think so,' said Dill.

'Did Yelsrap have all this trouble?' asked Parsley.

'Yelsrap?' repeated Dill, looking most surprised.

'That's "you know who" spelt backwards,' said Parsley menacingly. 'And he's about to invent a machine for doing away with dogs. Grrrrrr!

'Mind you,' said Parsley, addressing the imaginary friend he kept for the occasions when Dill suddenly disappeared, 'you don't really need a *machine* in Dill's case. Just a few well-chosen words. He's a nice chap, but he does go on about his bones. That's the only trouble with dogs. They're all the same.'

While he was talking, a thoughtful expression gradually came over Parsley's face. 'I suppose one could make a mechanical dog,' he mused. 'It wouldn't take much . . . Just a few cogs, an old bit of velvet and some whiskers . . . Any old scraps would do . . . It's not like a lion . . . Stir it all up and say a magic spell . . . I'd have one in no time at all. *And* it wouldn't keep on about bones all the time!'

Parsley was so pleased with his idea he hurried off at once to see if he could borrow Pashana Bedhi's chef's pot.

Pashana Bedhi was most surprised when he heard what was going on.

'You want to borrow my chef's pot?' he exclaimed. 'To make a *dog*?'

Parsley nodded.

'You are welcome to,' said Pashana Bedhi, 'but I warn you, please be careful. This is the pot I've cooked with all these years. If you are not very, very careful, you will end up with a *hot* dog.'

Lady Rosemary was even more worried when Parsley asked if he could borrow her old velvet hat. She looked at Parsley and then at the chef's pot and then at her hat.

'Is it some kind of game?' she asked.

'Well,' said Parsley. 'Yes and no.'

'If it's "yes",' said Lady Rosemary, 'then I must say I'm most unhappy. And if it's "no" then I must say I don't like the sound of it. I don't like the sound of it at all. I can't think what you wish to do with my old velvet hat.'

Aunt Mint, on the other hand, seemed only too pleased to let Parsley have some wool. Aunt Mint spent most of her time knitting and she always had a pile of odd bits of wool left over.

'Not that they're very suitable for a dog's whiskers,' she said when Parsley explained what he had in mind. 'They're bound to go soggy in the wet weather.'

'Not when I've finished with them they won't,' said Parsley confidently. 'You wait and see.'

And he hurried off to catch Sir Basil before he went out fishing.

'Me bedside clock?' repeated Sir Basil. 'Don't see what you want a bedside clock for. Lions don't have beds.'

And Bayleaf, the gardener, didn't seem best pleased either when he caught Parsley making off with his broom.

In fact, all in all, Parsley decided it wasn't easy being an inventor and he was glad he didn't have to do it for a living.

But he put all the bits and pieces into the chef's pot and then he got out his book and looked under spells to see if he could find a suitable one.

'Mix together,
One, two, three,'

he recited as he stirred the contents of the pot.

'Come on, chaps,
It's time for tea.'

He looked at the book doubtfully. 'I suppose they know what they're talking about!' He read the instructions a bit further. '"Close your eyes",' it said, '"and turn round six times . . . slowly."'

It was while Parsley was turning round and round with his eyes closed that Dill came on to the scene again.

'Good gracious!' he exclaimed. 'Whatever's going on? Poor old Parsley. Don't say he's feeling dizzy! It's probably all this inventing.'

'Four,' said Parsley, turning in almost a complete circle.

'Five,' he said, turning in a slightly smaller circle.

'Five and a half . . . Five and three-quarters . . . Six!'

When Parsley opened his eyes he was halfway round the next circle and to his surprise he saw what seemed like an exact replica of Dill standing in front of him.

'Eureka!' he cried. 'It's worked!'

He took a closer look. 'Who would have thought it?' he exclaimed. 'It looks just like Dill.'

'There, there,' said Dill, trying to humour him.

Parsley ran his paw over Dill's back. 'The same fur,' he said. He ran his other paw over Dill's face. 'The same whiskers. It's amazing!'

'Well, of course,' said Dill modestly. 'Some dogs have it – some haven't!'

'It not only looks like Dill,' said Parsley excitedly. 'It *sounds* like him as well. I think I'll patent it. I'll flood the world with mechanical dogs . . .'

'How about mechanical dogs with everlasting bones?' said Dill. 'It's an idea I've been working on. You just add water and . . .'

Parsley looked at his 'mechanical dog' with disgust.

'On second thoughts!' he exclaimed. 'I've changed my mind. It'll never catch on. It's too much like the real thing!'

Chapter 5

MR ONION AND SELF-DEFENCE

Parsley sniffed the air. 'Today,' he said, 'feels like a mystery day! There's a definite smell of mystery in the air.

'In fact,' he continued, 'it's so strong I must definitely do something about solving it.'

So he got out his book and began riffling through the pages. 'A for 'orses, G for goodness' sake,* J for oranges,** M for sis,*** Q for the cinema . . .****

'I've gone too far as usual,' sighed Parsley, and he went back to the Ms. M for *mystery*. And then he started to read.

'"One of the biggest mysteries at the present time",' he read, '"is what has happened to Mr Bayleaf's tin of brown paint."

* See page 30
** Sounds like 'Jaffa oranges' – part of a joke alphabet
*** Sounds like 'emphasis'
**** Sounds like 'queue for the cinema'

'This is a marvellous book,' said Parsley, addressing the empty air or anyone who happened to be within earshot. 'It really is. There's nothing it doesn't know about.'

And he hurried off to see Mr Bayleaf, the gardener.

Bayleaf was busy doing things in his greenhouse when Parsley arrived. On the path outside there was a log-sawing stand and what looked like a pile of sawn-off logs. There was also a dried-up paintbrush and . . . an empty tin of paint.

'I never doubted it for one moment,' said Parsley, examining the tin. 'Not for one moment did I doubt it.

'Did you know someone's been at your paint tin, Mr Bayleaf?' he called.

Bayleaf gave a start and then came to the greenhouse door. 'What's that?' he called. 'Someone's been at my paint?'

He hurried outside and joined Parsley. 'I'll 'ave 'im,' he exclaimed. 'Whoever it is, I'll 'ave 'im. I got that paint special to paint my log stand, I did. And now look at it. I'll . . . I'll . . .'

'I should save your breath for a start,' said Parsley. 'Here comes Constable Knapweed. You'll only have to say it all over again.'

'And I shall,' said Bayleaf. 'And I shall. Make no mistake about it.'

'Going . . . to paint . . . log . . . stand . . .' said Constable Knapweed as he listened to Bayleaf's tale of woe and wrote it down in his notebook at the same time. 'This paint,' he said briskly. 'What colour was it?'

'Blow the colour!' exclaimed Bayleaf impatiently. 'Whoever took it'll be coming back for a refill by the time you've got all that down.' He picked up the paintbrush and thrust it under Constable Knapweed's nose. 'Look at this. 'Tis going 'ard already!'

'It all 'as to go down in the proper order, Mr Bayleaf,' said the constable stolidly. He began writing again. 'Paintbrush . . . going . . . hard . . .'

'Now then!' He snapped his notebook shut. 'This is a serious matter. It may well be the work of a gang.'

'A *gang*?' exclaimed Bayleaf.

The constable nodded. 'We must all be prepared,' he said. 'I shall ask Mr Onion to give a lecture on the art of self-defence this afternoon.'

'A *gang*?' exclaimed Parsley. '*Self-defence*? I think I'll stay here and . . .' He looked over his shoulder as he dived behind some bushes. 'I do wish there weren't so many bushes in the

Herb Garden. You never know who might be hiding behind them!'

Parsley wasn't the only one to feel nervous about the possibility of a gang being at large in the Herb Garden.

The news spread quickly and that afternoon a large crowd assembled in the clearing near the greenhouse in order to hear Mr Onion deliver his lecture.

Apart from Parsley, and of course Constable Knapweed, there was Sir Basil and Lady Rosemary, Mrs Onion and all the Chives, Bayleaf and Sage the owl. In fact, the only one missing was Dill, and in the end they decided to start without him.

As Mr Onion marched on there was a round of applause, which faded away as Constable Knapweed held up his hand.

'Thank you,' said the constable. 'Thank you!' He cleared his throat. 'Now, as you all know, I've called this meeting so that Mr Onion can give a short talk on the art of self-defence . . .'

'Hear! Hear!' called Sir Basil. 'Jolly good idea. Nothin' like bein' prepared.'

Lady Rosemary gave him a sharp poke with her sunshade. 'Do be quiet, Basil,' she exclaimed. 'I can't hear what's goin' on.'

'Thank you, Lady Rosemary,' said Constable Knapweed. He motioned to one side. 'I will now give you . . . Mr Onion!'

As the applause rang out again Mr Onion stepped forward in smart military fashion and surveyed his audience.

'For this demonstration,' he announced, 'I shall require the assistance of one able-bodied volunteer from the audience . . .'

'Let me get at 'em!' shouted Bayleaf, pushing his way to the front. 'Just let me get at 'em. I'll show 'em. Arrh! Taking my paint!

'Twere a new tin.'

'Good man,' said Mr Onion. 'That's what I like to see. Now, one of the first rules to learn is what is known as the free-standing position . . . feet wide apart . . . arms hanging loosely by the sides . . . so that you can bend down and touch your toes . . .'

Having demonstrated what he meant by this Mr Onion stood to one side to let Bayleaf have a go.

'Mr Bayleaf!' he shouted. 'Touching the toes by numbers . . . begin. One, pause . . . two, pause . . . three.

'Very good. Very good indeed.

'Now, if you'd like to stand up again I will demonstrate the hip throw, assailants from behind for the use of.'

'You bloomin' well won't!' cried Bayleaf, clutching his back. He glared up from his bent-double position. 'I'm stuck! I been assailed all right. Right in my back! Seized up good and proper I be. Oh, arrrh!'

''Ard luck, Mr Bayleaf,' said Mr Onion. He cleared his throat. 'Er . . . while we await the arrival of my good lady wife with the embrocation, is there anyone else in the audience as would care to assist in demonstrating the 'ip throw?'

'Tu whit, tu I will!' hooted Sage.

'Er . . . thank you, Sage,' said Mr Onion doubtfully as Sage hopped into view.

'Now,' he continued when Sage had settled himself down, 'some of you may never 'ave given an owl a 'ip throw before, but if you ever 'ave cause to . . .' Mr Onion paused for a moment while he tried to get his arms round Sage's ample waist. 'But if you ever 'ave cause to,' he continued, grunting and straining, 'you may find yourself . . . up against . . . certain difficulties . . . like . . .'

Mr Onion let go of Sage and stood up, mopping his brow.

'Like trying to find the 'ips of certain fat owls what's got nothing better to do than sit up in their nests screeching all day,' he snorted.

'Tu whit, tu whoo!' hooted Sage, looking most offended.

'If you come against either of these two situations,' continued Mr Onion, ignoring both the groans from Bayleaf and Sage's shrieks, 'then the next best thing to use is what is known as the karate chop . . .'

He crossed to the wood-sawing stand and picked up one of the logs, which he carefully placed along the top between the two Vs.

'For the purpose of demonstrating the karate chop I 'ave taken an ordinary log which I 'ave placed in the sawing-stand and, which I will now proceed to break in two with a single blow from the side of my 'and.'

Rolling up the sleeve on his right arm Mr Onion stood back with his palm outstretched, fingers together and, holding it sideways on, brought it down with all the force he could muster squarely in the centre of the log.

For several seconds he hopped about the clearing with his hand clasped under his arm.

'Cor!' he cried. 'Dear, oh dear!
Oooooh! Owwwww! My word. Begging your pardon, Lady
Rosemary, but cor! My word. Ohhhh!' He glared at the sawing-
stand. 'Them logs must be made of concrete!'

It was while the excitement was at its height that Dill rushed
on. 'I'm sorry I'm late for the lecture, Mr Onion,' he called. 'Did
you start without me? I had rather a heavy lunch. I had this big
bone left over and it weighed a ton.'

Mr Onion stared at him suspiciously, all the pain momentarily
forgotten. 'You 'ad a bone left over?' he repeated. 'Left over
from *what*?'

'From being painted,' replied Dill patiently. 'You see I found
this tin of brown paint this morning, so I thought I would give all
my bones a coat to disguise them.'

Dill turned to the others. 'You never know who's about these
days and it's better to be safe than sorry. It worked jolly well too.
They look just like logs . . .' He broke off. 'I say, why's everyone
staring at me?'

'You may well ask,' said Parsley.

Mr Onion examined his hand.

'Demonstrations!' he exclaimed bitterly.

'I'm about to give one myself,' said Constable Knapweed. 'A little demonstration entitled "How to arrest a dog – double quick"!'

'I can lend you my disguise outfit if you like,' whispered Parsley as Dill hurried past. 'If you lie low for a while it may all blow over . . .'

But Dill had gone. He was giving his own demonstration as well . . . on how to disappear in record time.

A moment later Parsley followed suit and as he went he sniffed the air. 'At least it's got rid of the smell of mystery,' he said. 'Now everything smells of paint!'

Chapter 6

DILL'S TELEVISION

One day Parsley was taking a quiet stroll past Dill's kennel, thinking of nothing in particular, when he happened to glance up and saw a sight that made him jump so he nearly ended up where he'd started from.

For there on Dill's chimney, as large as life and twice as bold, was a television aerial!

Parsley could hardly wait to ring Dill's front door bell in order to see what it was all about. 'Fancy keeping it to himself!' he exclaimed. 'To think of all the programmes I might have missed.'

He rang the bell once, he rang it twice, and he was about to ring it a third time when the door suddenly opened.

'Hullo,' said Dill. 'Sorry I was a long time. I was just making some adjustments to my contrast. They're doing a documentary on bones on channel two this evening, and I want to make sure it's working properly.'

'Channel two!' exclaimed Parsley. He turned to address his imaginary friend – the one he often spoke to when Dill was around and he needed a sensible answer. 'You get the significance! Where there's a channel two there may well be a channel one!'

'You needn't think it's easy having two channels,' said Dill. 'Decisions – the whole time decisions. Mind you,' he continued, 'I must say the colour's first rate these days. It has to be seen to be believed.'

'*I'm* quite willing to believe it,' said Parsley as he made to enter Dill's kennel, 'if you'll show it to me.'

Dill hastily turned sideways on, blocking Parsley's way. 'Oh!' he exclaimed. 'Oh! Er . . . um . . . grrr . . . I . . . er . . . ahem . . . Yes . . . well . . .'

'Are you all right?' asked Parsley. 'Can I get you anything?' He turned back to his imaginary friend. 'I expect it's all this switching channels. It's bound to have an effect in time . . .

I tell you what,' he continued, 'you go to bed with a nice, warm bone. I'll watch the television and tell you all about it later.'

Parsley broke off as he suddenly realised he was talking to a closed door. 'He's gone!' he exclaimed bitterly. 'There's friendship for you. As soon as some dogs get television they don't want to know you. I can't imagine what the others'll say when they get to hear!'

And because he couldn't imagine what some of the other inhabitants of the Herb Garden *would* say, Parsley went off to hear for himself.

The first person he asked was Constable Knapweed and the constable quickly made it very clear how he felt about the matter.

Within seconds of hearing the news he was knocking on Dill's front door.

'It has come to my knowledge,' he said when Dill opened his door, 'that you are in possession of a television receiver for which there is no record of a licence having been issued. It is my duty to effect an entry in order to watch programmes and take notes.'

And in order to show that he meant business he took out his notebook and pencil.

'I'm sorry,' said Dill, barring the way, 'but a dog's kennel *is* his castle, and I feel it's my duty to close my door-bridge!'

And with that he slammed his door shut.

'Did you see that?' exclaimed Constable Knapweed, turning to Parsley. 'Did you see that?'

But Parsley had already gone to fetch Mr Bayleaf.

As it happened he needn't have bothered, for Bayleaf was already on his way to see Dill. He was clutching a piece of paper in his hand and he had a very cross expression on his face indeed.

''Ere, what's the meaning of this?' he exclaimed as Dill opened his door. ''Twere stuck to my lawnmower . . . "Please do not use during hours of viewing . . . on account of interference."'

Dill nodded. 'That's right,' he said. 'It tells you all about it in my instruction book. Lawnmower engines make grass grow all over television screens. They have to be suppressed!'

'Suppressed!' growled Bayleaf. 'I'll give him suppressed. 'E'll get suppressed if 'e don't watch out!'

The door opened again and Dill popped his head round the side. 'You can use it after eleven o'clock at night if you like,' he said. 'I don't usually stay up after then unless there's a good film on, and if there is I'll let you know well in advance.'

'Would you believe it?' snorted Bayleaf as the door closed again. He got down on his hands and knees and tried to peer through the letter box. 'If dogs 'ad been meant to watch television they'd 'ave been given square eyeballs. Besides, there's a programme on gardening I wants to see.'

Parsley hurried round to the side of the kennel in the hope of seeing through one of the windows, but the curtains were all tightly drawn.

'Isn't it frustrating?' he agreed. 'I wouldn't even mind a quick look at a test card.'

Constable Knapweed looked up from a knothole. 'If you ask me,' he said, 'there's something going on 'e don't want us to know about.'

Bayleaf put his shoulder to the door and when it didn't budge he gave a snort. 'I'm going to get my ladder,' he said. 'If the worst comes to the worst we'll flush 'im out.'

'Good idea, Mr Bayleaf,' said Constable Knapweed. 'While you're doing that I'll go and make out a search warrant. We're losing valuable viewing time.'

'Search warrant?' said Parsley, looking from one to the other. 'Ladder? I know a *much* better way. Watch me.'

And he walked straight up to the front door and rang the bell.

'Look,' said Dill impatiently when he opened it a moment later, 'I shall *never* get my picture adjusted properly if this goes on . . .'

Parsley coughed and stole a glance at the others. 'What would you say,' he began casually, 'if I told you I'd seen a pile of bones on the path?'

Dill jumped. 'What?' he exclaimed. 'Where?' And before Parsley had time to say any more he'd disappeared down the garden path as fast as his legs would carry him.

Parsley turned to the others. 'It's like taking candy from a babe,' he said. 'It really is. Follow me.'

As he led the way into Dill's kennel

Parsley looked around with interest. It wasn't often he was allowed inside and when his eyes grew accustomed to the gloom he saw, standing in a place of honour, a small television set.

'I say, how the rich do live,' he began, and then something about the television pulled him up with a start. It was quite an ordinary-looking set in a square box-like cabinet on legs. Much like any other television receiver, and yet, there on the screen, as large as life – in fact, twice as large as life – was a very familiar figure.

'Why, 'tis old Dill 'isself!' exclaimed Bayleaf. 'What's 'e doing on the television?'

'Don't say they've been doing a programme about him!' exclaimed Constable Knapweed. 'They must be short of material if they are.'

Parsley hurried over to the set. 'I'll soon fix *that*!' he cried. 'I'll change his channel. I'll . . .' An odd look came over his face as he pressed the buttons, for no matter which one he tried nothing happened. The picture remained exactly the same.

He took a closer look at it. 'It isn't even a *real* television set!' he exclaimed in disgust. 'It's an old cabinet with a photograph stuck to the screen. Of all the . . .'

'I can't find any bones!' gasped Dill as he rushed into the room. 'Were you pulling my legs?'

Parsley stared at him, for once at a loss for words.

'Was *I* pulling *your* legs?' he gasped. 'How can you run round in circles and say it? Making out you'd bought a television when all the time—'

'*Bought* one?' exclaimed Dill. It was his turn to look amazed. 'You must be joking. Catch *me* doing a thing like that. I shall wait and see if it catches on first.'

'Would you believe it?' said Parsley in disgust.

'Of all the nerve!' agreed Constable Knapweed.

'No wonder 'e didn't want anyone to see it!' snorted Bayleaf.

But Dill was staring at the screen. 'You may scoff,' he said, looking at his picture, 'but if they'd put programmes like that on they couldn't really fail. Think of the viewing figures it would have.'

He turned to the others. 'Do you like my picture? Isn't science wonderful? I could watch it all day, couldn't you? Wouldn't it be nice if they turned it into a series?'

Parsley took a deep breath. 'The answer to all those questions,' he said, 'is no, yes, and no, no, a thousand times no!'

'If you jump up and down with your eyes closed,' said Dill, 'it *almost* looks as if it's moving.'

In order to show what he meant Dill did several leaps into the air, but when he opened his eyes again everyone had gone.

'Speaking for myself,' said Parsley, amid general agreement as they made their way back home, 'I've had quite enough viewing for one day!'

✿Chapter...7

PARSLEY'S CAR

One day Parsley was out for a ramble when he nearly ran over a motor car.

It was that way round because the car was stationary at the time and very badly parked – right across one of the paths leading to Dill's kennel. On a corner as well, so that Parsley didn't see it until it was too late.

It was a very unusual sort of car. Not a bit like the ones he'd sometimes seen speeding along the road outside the Herb Garden. Although it had all the normal bits and pieces they somehow *looked* different. Even the horn was distinctly odd.

Instead of working it from a button in the middle of the steering wheel, or even on a stalk sticking out from underneath, it consisted of a large black bulb joined to a curly brass object, not unlike a trumpet.

It worked too! Parsley tried it several times. He put his mouth to it and squeezed. 'Honk! Honk! Honk! Honk!'

The third time he squeezed it he not only got a 'Honk! Honk!' but something else happened as well.

A strange-looking figure rose from behind the far side of the car. It was wearing a cloth cap and a silk scarf and it spoke.

'Good afternoon, sir,' it said. 'Can I help you?'

'Er . . . good afternoon,' said Parsley, playing for time. 'I . . . er . . . I was just browsing.'

'Are you interested in this model, sir?' asked the figure. 'It's a fine old specimen. You won't find another like it in a hurry.'

Parsley took a closer look at the salesman. It not only looked like Dill. It sounded like him as well. In fact, it *was* Dill.

'Where on earth did you get this?' he asked.

'My Uncle Mortimer left it to me,' said Dill. 'He passed on, you know.'

'I'm sorry to hear that,' said Parsley. 'I didn't even know he'd been ill.'

'Oh, he wasn't,' said Dill. 'He just passed on. He left me the car because the back wheel fell . . . er . . . ahem . . .' He hurried round to the back of the car and placed himself alongside one of the rear wings. 'Pardon me,' he exclaimed. 'Just an attack of my old complaint. I say, are you really interested?'

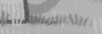

Parsley pricked up his ears. 'You mean – it's for sale?'

'If I can find a big enough . . . er . . . that is, someone big enough to appreciate the finer points of this magnificent specimen,' said Dill. 'This example of all that's best in mechanical engineering . . .'

While he was talking Dill ushered Parsley towards the front of the car and leant on one of the headlamps.

'The detachable headlamps . . .' he added hastily as one of them clattered to the ground.

'How much?' asked Parsley.

'Make me an offer!' exclaimed Dill eagerly. 'I can do easy payments if you like. Ten bones down and the rest over fifty years. You'll have many happy hours . . . meandering through the countryside . . . listening to the radio . . .'

Parsley peered at the dashboard. 'The radio?' he said. 'I can't see any radio.'

'You don't *see* radio,' said Dill. 'You listen to it.' He led the way back round the car and lifted up a

lid at the back. 'It's here in the seat – behind the cocktail cabinet.'

Parsley gazed over his shoulder. 'Cocktail cabinet?' he exclaimed. 'I don't call a tool box with a chicken feather inside a *cocktail* cabinet.'

'This *is* the Mark I model,' said Dill. 'I tell you, sir, if you buy this you won't just be buying a motor car – you'll be purchasing a work of art.'

'Does it go?' asked Parsley suspiciously.

'Does it go?' repeated Dill. '*Does it go?*' He gave a hollow laugh.

'Well,' said Parsley. 'Does it?'

'This car,' said Dill, 'has an engine like a sewing machine.'

He pressed the starter. 'Listen.'

'It sounds more like a threshing machine to me!' shouted Parsley above the roaring and the clanging and the banging. 'How about the tyres?'

'The tyres?' cried Dill. He jumped down from the seat and hastily planted himself at the back of the car again. 'I'm glad you mentioned those, sir. Very glad indeed. They're the latest treadless variety. No rough edges to slow you down on corners. They're so smooth you just carry straight on. You'll glide along on these tyres, sir.'

A dreamy expression came over Parsley's face as he listened to Dill talking. 'I must say the idea's very tempting,' he began.

'You'll never regret buying it, sir,' said Dill. 'You have my word.'

'That,' said Parsley, 'is the one thing that bothers me.'

'Why not try sitting in the driving seat for a moment, sir,' said Dill. 'Familiarise yourself with the controls. I'll just pop into my office and complete the formalities. Fill in the guarantee form . . .'

'By Jove!' said Parsley as he settled himself down. 'This is the life.' He pressed the horn bulb. 'Honk! Honk!'

He'd hardly finished his first honk when Dill came rushing back with a piece of paper and a pen in his mouth.

'Perhaps you'd just like to put your mark on here, sir,' he announced.

'That was quick,' said Parsley.

'Service with a laugh,' said Dill brightly.

'Don't you mean a smile?' asked Parsley.

Dill shook his head. 'I know what I mean,' he exclaimed knowingly.

'Hullo, hullo!' The familiar tones of Constable Knapweed rang out. 'What's going on here?'

He took out his notebook. 'I suppose you realise this is

a serious offence? 'Aving charge of a vehicle what is in an unroadworthy condition. To whit, minus a rear wheel!'

Parsley jumped out of the car in alarm. *'Minus a rear wheel?'* he repeated.

'I shall expect to see this put right before I get back,' intoned Constable Knapweed, *'or else . . .'*

'Fancy selling me a car without a rear wheel!' said Parsley bitterly as Constable Knapweed went on his way.

'You should have asked me about the optional extras,' replied Dill primly.

'I'll give you optional extras!' exclaimed Parsley. 'What about my guarantee?'

'I'm afraid it expired two minutes ago,' said Dill. 'I wish you'd come to me sooner. I'd take it back but there's no call for this sort of car just now. The bottom's dropped right out of the market.'

As he spoke he leant on the car and it fell over with a crash.

'It sounds as though the bottom's dropped out of my car as well,' said Parsley. 'Talk about a *bone-shaker*!'

'A bone-shaker?' Dill pricked up his ears. 'Uncle Mortimer didn't tell me it was one of those.'

He began running round and round in circles.

'Shall we go for a quick spin?' he asked excitedly. 'I'll get the spare wheel . . . It won't take a moment . . .'

'Isn't it amazing!' exclaimed Parsley, addressing the world in general as Dill busied himself with a hammer. 'Just mention the word "bone" and he's off like a shot.'

'Right!' called Dill. 'I've got the spare wheel on. All set?'

Parsley climbed into the driving seat. 'All set,' he called. 'Jump in. I'll press the starter. Ready?'

'Steady,' called Dill.

'Go!' cried Parsley.

Bracing himself, he took his paw off the clutch and leant forward ready to move away. He wasn't quite sure what happened next, but instead of going forward he found himself shooting backwards, only to end up seconds later against a nearby tree with a crash that seemed to jar every bone in his body.

'That's something else I forgot to mention,' said Dill sadly as he clambered out. 'You know that knob thing on top of the gear lever? The one that's got *forward* and *reverse* written on it?'

Parsley held up a small black object. 'You mean this?' he asked.

'It was on the wrong way round,' said Dill. 'You were in reverse.'

Parsley stared at him. 'I'll tell *you* something now,' he growled. 'Cars bring out the worst in people . . . and lions!'

'Do they really?' said Dill with interest. 'Fancy that!'

'Yes,' said Parsley. 'Normally quiet, inoffensive lions like me, for instance. They go right off dogs . . . especially dogs who set themselves up as car dealers! Grrrrrrdnight!'

⚘Chapter 8

PARSLEY'S BREAKDOWN

One morning, soon after he'd bought the car from Dill, Parsley woke and almost immediately afterwards he had A THOUGHT.

'Today,' he announced, addressing the world in general, 'today feels like a motoring day.'

It was such a strong feeling he even made up a little song about it, which he sang to himself.

> *'I rather feel today's a motoring day,*
> *With a little delay . . .*
> *I'll be on my way . . .'*

Parsley couldn't think of any more words for his song, so he sang the same verse several times over and then went to look for his car.

'I must say,' he announced again as he caught sight of the gleaming bodywork through the bushes. 'I must say I really do feel like a drive today. A nice, long drive in the country . . .'

He climbed into the driving seat and surveyed the interior. 'There's nothing like it, you know. The smell of old leather . . . the instruments . . .' He peered at the dashboard. 'Er . . . well . . . the instrument . . . er, the knob . . . The feel of the wind ruffling your whiskers . . . The smell of the hedgerows as they flash past . . .'

He reached for the knob on the dashboard.

'The soft purr of the engine as it roars into life . . .'

He pressed the knob and almost immediately there was a harsh grinding noise followed by a loud explosion followed by . . . nothing. Absolute dead silence . . .

'That's very strange!' exclaimed Parsley. 'Perhaps I'd better consult my book.'

So he climbed out of the car, opened his book – which always appeared as if by magic whenever he needed it – and began turning the pages.

'I wonder if it's under B for breakdowns,' he mused, 'C for cars, or L for lifts, thumbing . . . or even T for thumbing, lifts, lions for the use of?'

Parsley decided to try B for breakdowns first.

'Breakdowns,' it said. 'If your car breaks down why not try

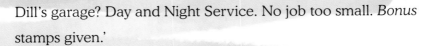

Dill's garage? Day and Night Service. No job too small. *Bonus stamps given.*'

Parsley stared at the pages as if he could hardly believe his eyes. 'If he writes in my book once more . . .' he spluttered, 'I'll . . . I'll . . . On the other hand . . .' He thought for a moment. 'I mean . . . there isn't another garage for miles. I suppose there's nothing for it.'

So he went round the back of the car and started to push it along the path past Bayleaf's greenhouse . . . along another path . . . round several shrubberies and on towards Dill's kennel.

'I've heard of horsepower,' he gasped, 'but this is ridiculous! If I'd known motoring was going to be this hard I would never have taken it up!'

As he drew near Dill's 'garage' there was a slight bump as the front wheels rode over a length of rubber tube, and almost immediately a bell started ringing.

The door to Dill's kennel burst open and Dill, dressed in a rather old and greasy pair of overalls, rushed out.

'Hullo!' he called. 'Have you got a puncture? Don't worry. I'll soon have it fixed!' And without more ado he hurled himself on to the nearest back tyre.

'Look!' cried Parsley as the wheel fell to the ground. 'I haven't got a puncture!'

There was a hiss of escaping air and Dill stood up. 'You have now,' he said.

Parsley raised his head. 'I can see I'm going to regret this!' he groaned. 'The trouble *happens* to be in the engine,' he explained, turning back to Dill.

Dill lifted off the bonnet and threw it to the ground.

'Let me have a listen,' he exclaimed, leaning over into the compartment. 'I'm good at engines. What I don't know about engines would fill a book.'

He took his head out from where the bonnet had been. 'It sounds all right to me,' he said. 'I don't think I've ever heard a quieter one.'

'That,' said Parsley, 'is because it isn't working.'

'There's a reason for everything in this world,' called Dill. He buried his head in the engine compartment again. 'Could you try turning the starting handle for a moment. There are a couple of loose wires here. I'll just try tying them together and see what happens.'

'I must say,' said Parsley, 'it's nice to be in the paws of a real expert. It gives you that feeling of confidence . . .'

All the same, on the basis of anything for a quiet life, especially where Dill was concerned, Parsley did as he was told. He went round the front of the car and began turning the starting handle. He turned and he turned, and it wasn't until he stood up in order to mop his brow that he noticed to his surprise something strange had happened to the back of the car. The hood was up.

'I see you've got the latest optional extra,' said Dill brightly when he noticed it too. 'Lion-assisted hoods. They're all the rage.'

'I shall be all the rage soon if I don't get my car fixed,' growled Parsley '*Try tying the wires together to see what happens indeed!*'

He pulled the handle out with a jerk and as he did so the hood came down and the radiator fell off.

'Careful!' said Dill as he dived under the car. 'That might have landed on someone's paw! I say,' he continued in a muffled voice, 'you haven't had your chimney swept lately!'

'Chimney?' repeated Parsley. 'What chimney?'

There was a loud crash and almost immediately

Dill reappeared holding a long length of pipe. 'This one!' he announced. 'The one that was holding up your engine.' He glanced down at the bits and pieces lying underneath the car. 'Fancy holding it in with a piece of old chimney pot. No wonder it wouldn't go!'

'That chimney pot,' said Parsley, between his teeth, 'happens to be the exhaust pipe!'

'Oh dear.' Dill threw it on the already growing heap of parts. 'It looked different under the car. Never mind . . . Have you seen my spanner anywhere?'

'If I had,' said Parsley, 'I wouldn't let you within a mile of it. You're bad enough with bare paws let alone a spanner.'

Dill lifted out the back seat and dumped it on the ground. 'Well, it must be somewhere,' he said. 'I had it when I came out.'

He lifted off the steering wheel and handed it to Parsley. 'Here, hold this a moment, will you? I'll just have another look underneath.'

Parsley stared at the object in his paws as Dill disappeared from view again. 'I've only been here two minutes,' he groaned, 'and look at it . . .'

''Ullo, 'ullo,' said a familiar voice. 'What's going on 'ere?'

Parsley turned to see Constable Knapweed staring at the scene over the top of his notebook. 'It's not what's going on that bothers me,' he said. 'It's what's coming off!'

'Coming off or going on,' said Constable Knapweed sternly, 'it makes no difference. This heap of junk is in the way and I want to see it moved.' As he spoke Constable Knapweed leant on the rear of the car. It fell over and then almost immediately rose into the air again. 'Look at that! It's in an unroadworthy condition.'

'For once,' said Parsley, 'I'm not arguing. This car isn't even in a footpathworthy condition.'

'Mind you,' said Constable Knapweed as he pushed the back of it down and then watched while it rose into the air, 'I'll say one thing for it. It's got good springing. Just look at that!' He pushed the back down several more times and each time it rose into the air again like a yo-yo. 'They knew how to make cars in those days!'

'Those springs,' said Dill as he crawled out from under the car, rubbing his head, 'happen to be in here. My head doesn't know whether it's coming or going.'

'Hummph!' said Constable Knapweed. 'Well, I've said it once and I'm not saying it again. Either this gets moved or there'll be a few names going down in my notebook . . . beginning with the Ps and ending with you know what . . .' And with that he moved on his way.

'Er . . . I suppose I'd better be going too,' said Dill carelessly. 'Cheerio. See you tomorrow.'

'Come back!' called Parsley. 'You can't leave things like this. You got me into this mess. Now you get me out. Just look at it. Bits and pieces everywhere.'

'I'm sorry,' said Dill. 'It's early closing today.' He bent down and picked a large object off the ground. 'By the way, you won't want this old can, will you?'

'Old can?' repeated Parsley. 'What old can?'

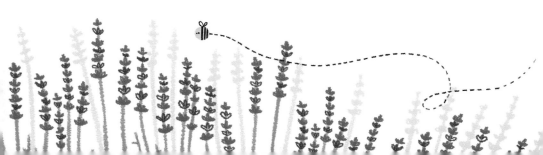

'I found it under the car,' said Dill. He held it up to his nose and gave a sniff. 'It pongs a bit, but I'll give it a good clean out. It'll do to keep my bone reserves in.'

'That old can,' said Parsley, consulting a diagram in his book, 'happens to be the *petrol tank*.'

He grabbed it away from Dill and held it upside down. 'And it's empty! No wonder my car wouldn't go! Fancy taking it all to bits just to find this out!'

'I'm not infallible,' said Dill. 'I said I was wrong once and I was proved right. Besides, every dog has his woof day!'

'It's yours today all right!' said Parsley. He looked around for help. 'Anybody want to buy a kit of parts for a car?' he called.

'I say, that's a good idea,' exclaimed Dill. 'I've been thinking of starting up a build-your-own-car business myself.'

He ran round and round the remains of Parsley's car, peering at it as he went.

'It's a lovely little runner. Only ten to six on the clock! Complete with working horn . . . "Beep! Beep!" Has to be seen to be believed!'

Parsley gave a sigh. 'I know someone else who's like that!' he exclaimed as he curled up on the seat. 'And even then it's hard to believe sometimes.' He gave another deep sigh as he closed his eyes. 'It was such a nice day for a ride in the country too!'

❧Chapter 9

DILL'S *WHO'S WHO* ENTRY

One day, soon after he'd given up motoring, Parsley was out for a walk in the Herb Garden when he came across Dill, lying fast asleep under a bush.

By his side there was a piece of paper with some writing on it, and alongside that was a rather blunt pencil with a chewed end.

Now there's nothing more interesting than reading something you're not really supposed to read – like a piece of paper that has been written on by a dog who is fast asleep under a bush, especially a dog like Dill, and Parsley needed no second thoughts on the matter.

Dill is A dog.
He lives in the Herb
Garden. HE is
moDest... kind..
GENEROUS to a fault..
cheeRful... a loyal
FRiend... FRightened
of nothing... noble...
uPRight...

105

He picked up the paper and settled himself down for a good read.

'"Dill",' he read, '"is a dog. He lives in the Herb Garden. He is modest . . . kind . . . generous to a fault . . . cheerful . . . a loyal friend . . . frightened of nothing . . . noble . . . upright . . ."'

Parsley read through the paper several times just to make sure his eyes weren't deceiving him and then peered at the figure still fast asleep beside him.

'Good gracious!' he exclaimed. 'You wouldn't think one small dog, who's mostly fur anyway, could have such a large imagination.' He gave Dill a passing poke with his paw. 'I wonder where he keeps it?'

'Grrrrrowwwww!' shrieked Dill as he leapt into the air.

And 'Grrrrrr!' he repeated several minutes later when he'd calmed down. 'You made me jump,' he complained, peering out through the bushes to see who'd been attacking him. 'I was having such a nice dream.'

'I should think you were,' exclaimed Parsley, holding up the sheet of paper. 'Did you write this?'

Dill put on his modest expression. 'You like it?' he asked. 'You think it's good?'

'Like it?' repeated Parsley. 'Did you say *like* it?'

'It's my entry for *Who's Who*,' said Dill. 'Just in case they ever ask me. I always think it's as well to be prepared for these things.'

'I think it's terrible,' said Parsley. 'I mean, if one half of it was true it wouldn't be so bad, but when none of it is . . .'

'Not *true*?' broke in Dill. 'What do you mean, not true?'

'Well,' said Parsley, 'you only have to read it.' He glanced down at the paper again. '"Dill is a dog. He lives in the Herb Garden" . . . I suppose it's all right up to there. I mean, you can't really argue about that. Good factual stuff. Neatly written. Ten out of ten for that.'

'Thank you,' said Dill.

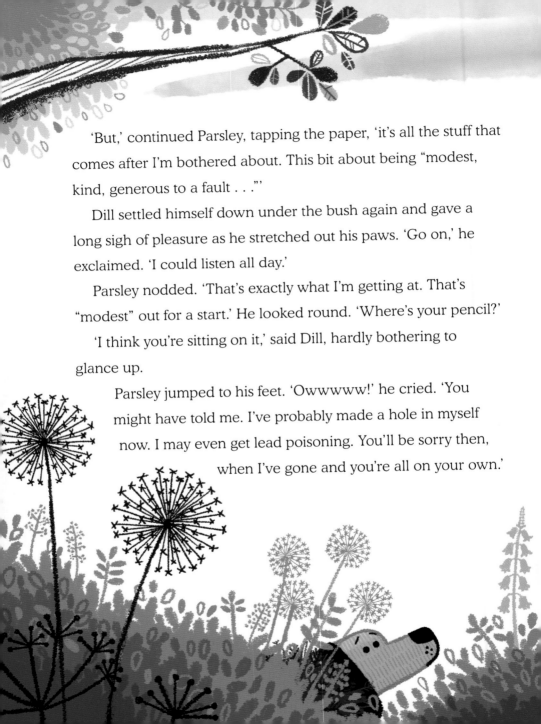

'But,' continued Parsley, tapping the paper, 'it's all the stuff that comes after I'm bothered about. This bit about being "modest, kind, generous to a fault . . ."'

Dill settled himself down under the bush again and gave a long sigh of pleasure as he stretched out his paws. 'Go on,' he exclaimed. 'I could listen all day.'

Parsley nodded. 'That's exactly what I'm getting at. That's "modest" out for a start.' He looked round. 'Where's your pencil?'

'I think you're sitting on it,' said Dill, hardly bothering to glance up.

Parsley jumped to his feet. 'Owwwww!' he cried. 'You might have told me. I've probably made a hole in myself now. I may even get lead poisoning. You'll be sorry then, when I've gone and you're all on your own.'

'No, I shan't,' said Dill unfeelingly. 'It serves you right. Sitting on other people's pencils. You should have looked before you sat down. Look before you leap – that's what I always say.'

Parsley picked up the pencil and drew a firm line across the page. 'Right,' he said, 'that gets rid of "kind".' He looked up. 'May I borrow one of your bones?'

'No,' said Dill firmly. 'I've only got fifteen left to last the week.'

Parsley drew another line across the page. '"Generous to a fault"!' he exclaimed. 'Out!'

He stared at his friend. 'I don't know how you could have written all this stuff. I really don't. There won't be much of it left soon. Now, where were we . . . "cheerful"?'

Dill pursed his lips in an attempt to whistle, but all he could manage was a kind of hissing noise like a kettle on the boil.

'Cheerful?' said Parsley. '*Cheerful?* It sounds more like a pricked balloon going down on a wet Sunday afternoon in Skegness.'

'Well, you try being cheerful when all your illusions are being shattered one by one,' said Dill. 'I've a good mind to tell Constable Knapweed.'

'"Cheerful" . . . *out*,' said Parsley, running his pencil across the page. '"Loyalty" . . . *out*! I shall need a pencil sharpener soon at this rate.'

'Well,' said Dill, 'at least no one can say I'm not brave. When I think back to some of the things I've done in the past, the Scarlet Pimpernel doesn't come close.'

'Your memory isn't too good either,' said Parsley.

'What do you mean?' asked Dill.

Parsley leant over and lifted up the flap over one of Dill's ears. 'Booooo!' he roared suddenly.

Dill leapt into the air as if he'd been fired from a cannon and began running round and round in circles as if his tail were on fire.

'What did you do that for?' he gasped when he came to a halt at long last. 'Making me jump!'

'"Frightened of nothing"!' read Parsley meaningly. 'Scarlet Pimpernel indeed! More like the Scarlet Pimple!' He glanced down at the page. 'I shall be running out of pencil soon. "Noble" . . . we'd better cross *that* out. "Upright" . . . that can go as well!'

Dill turned over on his back and lay for a moment with his paws in the air.

'All right,' he said at last. 'I pass.'

'Would you like me to read it back?' asked Parsley. 'It won't take long and it's good for a laugh.'

'Grrrrrrmpphhhhhhh!' snored Dill, closing his eyes.

'"Dill",' said Parsley, reading from the paper, '"is a dog. He lives in the Herb Garden". Yes. Yes, I think that just about sums it all up. You can't say fairer than that. In fact, there's nothing more *to* be said.

'Mind you –' a thoughtful expression came over Parsley's face as he gazed at the paper – 'this needn't be entirely wasted. It *could* still be used. It only needs one or two words changed here and there. Like "lion" instead of "dog". Yes, that sounds better. "Parsley is a lion. He lives in the Herb Garden. He is modest . . . kind . . . generous to a fault . . . cheerful . . . a loyal friend . . . frightened of nothing . . ."'

'Wuff!' said Dill suddenly. 'Wuff! Wuff!'

It was Parsley's turn to jump in the air. He looked round at Dill. 'Of all the . . . what on earth did you do that for? Wuffing at me like that!'

'You have to take the wuff with the smooth,' said Dill. 'Besides, it's a wise lion who sees himself as others see him.'

'Perhaps you're right,' said Parsley. 'Anyway, who wants to be one of the whos in *Who's Who*?'

'Only someone who's "modest, kind, generous to a fault, cheerful, a loyal friend, frightened of nothing, noble and upright",' said Dill.

Parsley nodded. 'Come to think of it,' he said, 'there aren't many of us left now!'

PART 2

Chapter 10

THE SOUND OF THE SEA

One day Parsley the lion was out for a walk in the Herb Garden when he came across an enormous seashell lying slap bang in the middle of one of the paths.

After peering at it from behind a bush for a minute or two he crept closer and closer towards it on his stomach, gently eased up one corner in order to make sure there was nothing hiding underneath and then decided to consult his book.

'I am quietly confident,' he announced to himself, and to anyone else who happened to be within earshot, 'that under "sea", *shells* will lie the answer!'

Parsley had never known his book to let him down. Between its covers it had everything about everything, and there, sure enough, just where he had said it would be, was a picture of a large shell exactly like the one he'd found.

It was called a 'conch' shell, and the book went on to say that if you blew into it you could make a noise like a foghorn. It also said that sometimes, if you put your ear to it, you could even hear the sound of the sea.

Parsley tried listening, first at one end of the shell and then at the other, but he couldn't hear a thing, so he decided to try blowing into it instead and to his surprise a noise just like a ship's siren came out the other end.

He gave it a second blow, and then another. 'Hmmmmmmmmph! Hmmmmmmmmmph!' It really was most impressive.

He was just in the middle of his third go when there was a bark and Dill the dog hurried on to the scene.

'Did you call?' he panted. 'I say, what have you got there?'

'A conch shell,' said Parsley carelessly, breaking off in mid-honk.

'Can you eat it?' asked Dill eagerly.

'Can you eat it?' repeated Parsley. *'Can you eat it?'*

'Well?' demanded Dill. 'Can you?'

'No,' said Parsley firmly. 'You *can't!*' He put his mouth to it again and blew. 'But you can use it as a horn.' Then he sat down on top of it. 'And it makes a very good seat. And it says in my book that if you listen hard enough you can sometimes hear the sound of the sea.'

'Can you really?' exclaimed Dill. 'May I have a go?'

Parsley gave a superior sort of laugh. 'If you like,' he said. 'But I'm afraid it's not really meant for dogs. You have to be particularly sensitive.' He consulted his book again as he changed places with Dill. 'It says so here. "It is only given to a lucky few," it says, and if I can't hear anything I'm sure you—'

'Do be quiet a moment!' Dill's tail began to wag violently to and fro as he put his ear to the shell. 'I say, it's jolly good, isn't it?

It sounds as though it's high tide.' He looked up. 'What were you saying just now?'

'Er . . . nothing,' said Parsley. 'Er . . . may I have it again for a moment?'

Pushing Dill to one side, he put his head to the shell.

'Lovely, isn't it?' said Dill.

'Er . . . yes,' said Parsley.

'I mean, it really makes you feel as if you're there,' said Dill. 'The sound of the waves crashing against the rocks . . . the seagulls crying . . . the ships' sirens . . .'

'*Do* be quiet,' said Parsley. 'I'm trying to concentrate.'

'I thought it was rather loud,' said Dill. 'I had a job to hear what you were saying.'

'Oh, fiddlesticks!' snorted Parsley crossly, and putting his mouth to the shell he gave it a hard blow. 'It makes you want to have a good, long honk!'

'Here comes Constable Knapweed,' said Dill as the sound of the horn echoed and re-echoed round the Herb Garden before gradually dying away. 'Perhaps he'd like to have a go?'

'Hullo, hullo!' Constable Knapweed took out his notebook as he drew near. 'What's going on here?' He peered at the conch shell standing in the middle of the path. 'I hope you've got a licence for that there contraption.'

He looked down suspiciously as Dill put his ear to the shell. 'You need a licence for singing, dancing *and* blowing seashells in the Herb Garden.'

'Shh!' said Dill.

'What's that?' growled the constable. 'Did I hear you say "*Shh*"?'

Dill jumped to his feet in alarm. 'I'm sorry!' he exclaimed. 'I didn't really mean to shush you up, but I thought I heard someone calling for help. It was only a boatman. "Come in, number twenty-nine!" he said.'

Constable Knapweed took out his pencil, licked the end and began writing. 'Come in . . . number twenty . . . nine,' he repeated slowly. ''Ere, are you pulling my leg, young Dill?'

Dill ran round and round in a couple of circles while he considered the matter. 'It may have been thirty-nine,' he said. 'It's a bit difficult to tell with all the other noises.'

'Other noises?' said Constable Knapweed suspiciously. '*What* other noises?'

'It's a conch shell,' explained Parsley. 'It says in my book that if you listen hard enough you can hear the sea.'

'But you need to be sensitive,' said Dill. 'It said that in the book as well.'

Constable Knapweed snapped his notebook shut. 'Why didn't you tell me that in the first place?' he exclaimed. 'Here, let me have a go.'

Removing his helmet he knelt down and put his ear to the shell.

'Isn't it nice,' said Dill dreamily. 'It makes you want to go for a paddle . . . or build a sandcastle.'

'I've 'eard louder,' said Constable Knapweed gruffly. He stood up and gave the others a stern look. 'Anyway, I don't know as I approve of these goings-on. I'm in the middle of my rounds at the moment, but I want to see that there shell moved by the time I get back or . . . or else . . .'

'I say,' said Dill as Constable Knapweed continued on his rounds, 'he's not in a very good mood, is he?' He bent down to

the shell again. 'I can't understand some people. You'd think hearing the sea like that would make them feel cheerful and full of beans.'

Dill's tail began to wag again. 'That sounds like the *QE2* going out!' he exclaimed. 'She's blowing her siren. There goes the gong for afternoon tea. I could listen to this all day.'

Parsley tried his best to put on a bored expression. 'I suppose it's all right if you like that sort of thing,' he said. 'But once you've heard one ship's siren you've heard the lot.'

'There's no need to go on holiday if you have one of these,' called Dill. 'Can I book up for next year?' He broke off as the familiar sound of a squeaking wheelbarrow drew near.

A moment later Bayleaf, the gardener, ground to a halt beside them.

''Ere!' he called. 'What's all this? What you be doing with that there shell?'

'Listening to the sea,' said Dill carelessly.

'Listening to the sea?' repeated Bayleaf.

'You can have a go if you like,' said Dill. 'Only I should hurry up if I were you. I think the tide's on the turn.'

Bayleaf removed his hat. 'I don't mind if I do,' he exclaimed. 'I don't know when I heard the sound of the sea last. Not since I were a lad . . .'

'I shouldn't get too worked up,' broke in Parsley as Mr Bayleaf got down on his hands and knees to have a listen. 'It's not all it's cracked up to be.'

'Arrh!' said Bayleaf after a moment or two.

Parsley gave a start. 'You can *hear* it?' he asked.

'Well,' said Bayleaf, 'course, t'ain't like it were when I was a lad. Nothing b'ain't be the same these days . . .'

'But isn't it wonderful?' said Dill. 'Don't you feel refreshed? Full of the joys of spring?'

Bayleaf stood up. 'No, I don't,' he said crossly. ''Tis all right for those what 'as nothing better to do, but I 'as my work . . .' He grasped the handles of his barrow. 'And if you asks me there's some as would be better employed using their paws 'elping in the garden instead of playing around . . .'

Dill looked offended as Bayleaf disappeared from view, still muttering to himself. 'What *is* the matter with everyone today?' he asked. 'You'd think they would be grateful.'

He bent down to the shell again. 'You know, it's just like being on a desert island.' He gave a deep sigh of contentment. 'I must say it's nice to be sensitive. Think of all the poor creatures there must be in the world who probably couldn't hear a thing.'

Parsley gazed up at the sky for help. 'I daren't tell him,' he murmured. 'It's hopeless. We should never hear the last of it.'

'I say, come and have

another listen,' called Dill. 'I do believe I can hear the cry of the Great Black-backed Gull!'

'Great Black-backed Gull indeed!' snorted Parsley. He put his head down beside Dill's in one last attempt. 'Doesn't it make you sick?'

'Well?' said Dill. 'Can *you* hear it?'

'No!' exclaimed Parsley in disgust. 'I can't. But I'm about to hear *something*.'

'What's that?' asked Dill with interest.

Parsley put his lips to the shell and blew as hard as he could. 'That!' he said. 'It's time for tea. There's nothing like a good blast for making you feel hungry!'

Chapter 11

HOLIDAY TIME

'It's just the day for going
Down to the sea,
I'll leave about three.
I might take my tea.'

Parsley's voice, loud and clear, rang round the Herb Garden. In fact, it was so loud and clear it even woke Dill, who hurried round as fast as he could in order to see what was going on.

The sight that met his eyes caused him to skid to a stop, blinking with astonishment, for it seemed as though Parsley was surrounded by the entire contents of several chemist's shops, a drapery and a general store all rolled into one.

There were bits and pieces everywhere.

Fishing nets, suitcases, carrier bags, several bottles of brownish-coloured liquid, bathing costumes, a tent, towels, a lifebelt . . . the list was endless.

'What *are* you doing?' gasped Dill with interest.

Parsley looked up. 'I'm thinking of going on holiday,' he said carelessly, raising his sunglasses for a moment to make sure it really was Dill he was talking to. 'Just getting everything ready. All the essentials . . . suntan lotion . . . sunshade . . . sunglasses . . . sunhat . . .'

'You're thinking of going somewhere sunny?' asked Dill.

'Uh-huh,' said Parsley, ticking off a few more items on his list. 'Bathing costume . . . towel . . . lifebelt.'

Dill sat down to watch. 'I rather fancy Buenos Aires myself,' he said dreamily. 'It sounds a nice sort of place.'

'Everybody goes there,' said Parsley. 'I want to get away from it all. An island somewhere. With parasols and palm trees and . . .'

'Where *are* you going?' asked Dill, idly picking up a bottle.

'*That*,' said Parsley, 'is a good question.'

'I know it's a good question,' said Dill.

'The point is . . .' He smacked his lips. 'I say, this suntan lotion tastes jolly good . . .'

'You're not supposed to *drink* it!' exclaimed Parsley, snatching the bottle away from him. 'Good gracious! You'll make your insides go funny.'

'You still haven't answered my question,' said Dill. 'Where are you going for your holiday?'

Parsley sat down and scratched his head. 'I don't know,' he said. 'I just don't know. At least, I know where I *want* to go. I'm not sure how I'm getting there.'

He glanced up as a distant drone came from somewhere high overhead. 'Doesn't it make you sick!' he growled. 'Everyone's flying off to faraway places and here we are . . . stuck in the Herb Garden!'

'Perhaps you could ask Sage to fly you?' said Dill

hopefully. 'You could make a sort of basket
to hang underneath him and ...'

'Sage?' exclaimed Parsley. 'You must be joking. He's never
been outside the Herb Garden in his life. Look at him . . .' He
nodded towards a nest high in a nearby tree. From somewhere
inside there came the rumble of a muffled snore. 'He's got the
sound effects off all right – it's like a jumbo jet taking off. But as for
carrying me *and* all my luggage . . . he'd never make it. And if you
think I'm sitting on his back while he hops all the way you're very
much mistaken.'

Dill closed his eyes. 'It must be nice to be able to fly,' he said. 'I
don't see why we can't really. I mean . . . if someone like Sage can
do it . . .'

Parsley jumped to his feet. 'You're right!' he exclaimed. '*You are
absolutely right.* I shall consult my book this very instant.'

And as luck would have it, on the very first page Parsley
found what he was looking for. There was a picture of
a 'bird-man'. Dressed from head to toe in white
overalls, he had an enormous pair of paper wings

fastened to his outstretched arms, and he looked as if he were about to jump from the top of a very high cliff.

He called Dill over. 'Look! There it is – right before your very eyes. A plain, ordinary, common or garden two-legged human man – just like Sir Basil, or Bayleaf, or Constable Knapweed . . . or Mr Onion . . . or . . . well . . .' Parsley hesitated for a moment. 'Perhaps not like any of *them* . . . but a human-type man nonetheless.'

'Come on,' said Dill. 'What are you waiting for?'

'The word "go",' said Parsley. 'That's all. Just the word "go".'

'I'll give you a wing,' called Dill as he hurried on ahead through the undergrowth. 'In fact, I'll give you two wings!'

A short while later and they were ready. Parsley, equipped with sunhat, sunglasses, sunshade and an enormous pair of paper wings, balanced himself precariously on top of Mr Bayleaf's greenhouse, while Dill settled himself on the ground below armed with the book.

He ran his paw down the page. 'Monday . . . Tuesday . . . Wednesday . . . Thursday . . . ah, there we are . . . Flyday.' He put on a strong American travel-film-type accent. 'Since early days man has always had a desire to conquer space.

To fly. One of his earliest attempts was with paper wings . . .
jumping from a high building . . .'

'*Do* hurry up,' called Parsley. 'I can't hold on much longer.
I think the altitude's affecting me. Besides, I've read all that
before.'

'All right,' said Dill. 'Get ready for take-off. Have a nice time.
Don't forget to write.'

'I'll send you a card,' called Parsley. 'With a picture of the
hotel as seen from my surfboard.'

'And some rock,' called Dill. 'Don't forget the rock. See if you
can get some shaped like a bone.'

'I'll try,' called Parsley. 'Er . . . talking of sweets, chocks away!'

He flapped his wings hopefully and then, looking down,
hurriedly closed his eyes. 'What do I do now?' he called.

'I suppose you have to jump,' said Dill vaguely. He consulted
the book again. 'There's a sort of note at the bottom. "See page
twenty-three," it says.'

'Oh, for goodness' sake!' cried Parsley. 'What a time to start reading notes.' He closed his eyes tightly and began flapping his wings as hard as he could. *'Au revoir!'*

'Au revoir!' called Dill as Parsley leapt into space. And 'Oh dear!' he cried as a violent crash shook the ground.

He hurried up to where Parsley was struggling to free himself from the wreckage. 'I've just found the footnote,' he announced. 'It says, "Most of these early attempts were doomed to failure. Especially when attempted by lions!"'

'*Now* he tells me!' groaned Parsley as he climbed shakily to his feet.

'I say!' broke in Dill excitedly. 'I've found something else. Look!'

Parsley examined himself carefully to make sure nothing was missing. 'If it's anything to do with jumping off greenhouses,' he growled, 'I don't wish to know about it.'

'Listen,' said Dill. 'It has always been believed that dragons can fly . . .'

'*Dragons?*' Even Parsley sounded impressed. 'You mean . . . like Tarragon?'

'That's what it says here,' replied Dill. 'There's even a picture of one.'

'There's room for two on a dragon,' said Parsley thoughtfully, '. . . standing. Would you like to come too?'

'Would I like to?' cried Dill. He ran round and round in circles for a moment or so at the very thought. 'Lead me to him,' he panted as he skidded to a halt at last. 'Just lead me to him.'

Tarragon was as enthusiastic as the others when he heard the news. 'We're going flying?' he exclaimed. 'How exciting! I don't know when I did any flying last. In fact, I don't think I've ever really done any before at all.'

'Oh!' Parsley's face fell and he exchanged a hurried glance with Dill. 'Oh! Er . . . well, in that case . . .'

'It says something in your book about practising a few circuits and bumps first,' broke in Dill.

'Circuits and *bumps*?' repeated Parsley. 'I don't like the sound of that very much.'

'It only means taking off and then landing again without bothering to stop,' explained Dill.

'In that case I definitely don't like it,' said Parsley.

'What goes up *must* come down,' said Dill.

'That,' said Parsley, 'is exactly what I'm afraid of.' He turned to Tarragon, who had been listening to the conversation with interest, smoke already coming from his nostrils in a steady stream as he got ready for the big event. 'I tell you what, just do a couple of circuits round Sage's nest first. We'll stay here and check the bumps when you get back.'

'Just as you like,' said Tarragon. 'Only hurry up. My smoke rings are getting rather worrying.'

'Right,' said Parsley briskly. 'Stand by for take-off.'

'Left wing down a bit,' called Dill.

'Ready . . .' said Parsley.

'Steady . . .' cried Dill excitedly.

'Go!' shouted Parsley.

Tarragon was more than ready. With a flash and a roar he was on his way. In fact, he was almost out of sight before Parsley had finished saying 'go'.

'Good gracious!' exclaimed Parsley. 'That was quick. If he goes that fast we shall be back from our holiday before the tide comes in.'

For the second time that morning the ground shook and there was a loud crash from somewhere near at hand, followed by an ominous tinkle of breaking glass.

'I think he's back already,' said Dill. 'That sounded like one of those bumps to me.'

'And I'll give you just one guess as to where it was too,' said Parsley gloomily. 'Listen!'

Mr Bayleaf's voice floated across the air. "Ere what's going on?' he shouted. 'Look at my greenhouse!'

Parsley and Dill crept through the undergrowth and peered out at the scene. But when they saw the look on Bayleaf's face as he surveyed the remains of his greenhouse they almost wished they hadn't.

'If dragons 'ad meant to fly,' snorted Bayleaf, helping Tarragon to his feet, 'they'd 'ave been given wings in the first place. And not made of paper neither. Whose idea *was* this? As if I didn't know!'

'Well,' said Tarragon sadly. 'It's a long story, Mr Bayleaf . . .'

'I've got all the time in the world,' said Bayleaf. 'All the time in the world. And I don't doubt Constable Knapweed 'as as well.'

Parsley and Dill looked at each other and then crawled quietly on all fours back to the bushes again.

'What we need,' said Parsley, 'is a good liar.'

'Don't you mean a lawyer?' asked Dill.

'I know what I mean,' said Parsley. 'Come on, I have a feeling it's going to be "holidays at home" this year – repairing greenhouses!'

✿Chapter 12

LOOKING INTO THE FUTURE

One day Dill was out for a ramble in the Herb Garden when he came across Parsley behaving in a very strange way.

'You're behaving in a very strange way!' he called.

But Parsley didn't take a scrap of notice. He was lying on his stomach peering at a silver ball of the kind you sometimes see hanging on Christmas trees – only much larger – and he was reading from his book.

As Dill drew nearer he stopped to listen.

'People,' said Parsley, 'whose birthday lies between the twenty-first of April and the twenty-first of May, were born under Taurus the bull.'

He looked up. 'Good gracious! Fancy that! If I'd known I wouldn't have had a minute's peace.'

Dill grew more and more impatient. 'What *are* you doing?' he repeated. 'Playing football? May I be centre-forward?'

Parsley gave him a withering look. 'Playing *football*?' he repeated. 'This isn't a *foot*ball. This is a *crystal* ball . . . for telling fortunes.'

'May I have a go?' cried Dill excitedly. 'Perhaps it'll tell me where my next bone is coming from?'

Parsley stood up. 'All right,' he said. 'But don't get too worked up. And don't go breathing heavily all over it. It's only just been cleaned.'

'I'll try and contain myself,' said Dill. 'But it's a bit difficult with breath. It's got to come out some time. And if I keep it all bottled up it's twice as bad.' He peered at the ball. 'I say, isn't this good?'

Parsley gave a start. 'You mean you can actually *see* something?' he exclaimed.

'Yes,' said Dill. 'A tall dark figure with silken whiskers. A handsome devil if ever I saw one.'

'That doesn't sound like Constable Knapweed,' said Parsley. 'Or Bayleaf come to that.

'Here, let *me* have a look,' he exclaimed as Dill stood up.

'I'm afraid it's gone now,' said Dill sadly. 'I think I must have been looking at my own reflection.'

'I need a handkerchief as well as patience when you're around,' growled Parsley. He blew on the ball a couple of times and then rubbed it with his paw. 'I have a feeling my ball needs cleaning again before it tells me any more fortunes.'

Dill sat up on his hind legs. 'How about paws?' he asked. 'Do you think you could read the future in my paws?'

Parsley glanced at Dill's nearest paw with a look of distaste. 'I don't know about your future,' he said. 'Your past doesn't look too good to me. You were either born under a cloud or you've just stepped in some mud.'

'*You* don't have to dig for bones,' said Dill. 'It isn't easy, you know.

Especially when there aren't any to be found.' He turned round. 'Try the other paw.'

Parsley gave a shudder. 'No, thank you,' he said. 'One's enough.' And then he looked down at his own paw. 'Anyway, mine says I ought to go for a long walk . . . starting *now*!'

'May I play with your ball?' asked Dill as Parsley turned to go.

'Help yourself,' said Parsley.

As Parsley disappeared up the garden path Dill had another look at the book.

It was already opened at the F for fortunes section.

'"To tell fortunes",' it said, '"all you need is somewhere quiet and a crystal ball."'

Dill peered at the ball. 'One out of two isn't bad,' he said. 'And before I'm very much older I shall make it two out of two. I'll have this crystal-ball-gazing business tied up before you can say ABRACADA– Er, well, before very long!'

There was a cunning gleam in Dill's eye as he hurried back to his kennel in order to prepare for his part. And when he returned a few minutes later, complete with some rope, an old sheet and a large notice advertising his services, there was an even brighter gleam. Dill had an idea in the back of his mind.

It was an idea that had to do with bones. And where bones were concerned Dill wasn't the sort of dog to let the grass grow under his feet.

It only took a few minutes' work with a piece of rope between two trees and the sheet and he was in business.

The first customer on the scene was Constable Knapweed.

Constable Knapweed was doing his rounds of the Herb Garden when he came across Dill's 'tent' and he was about to investigate the matter when he saw the notice outside.

YOUR FUTURE IS IN MY PAWS, it said. DOCTOR DILL SEES ALL. KNOWS ALL. MODERATE FEES.

Not even Constable Knapweed could resist a small peep into the future, and he was soon sitting beside Dill.

Dill peered hard at the crystal ball. 'I see a tall, distinguished-looking gentleman in blue,' he began. 'Carrying a large pile of bones.'

Constable Knapweed peered over Dill's shoulder. 'Bones?' he repeated. 'I can't see any bones.'

Dill hastily moved round to the other side of the ball.

'I'm not surprised,' he said. 'You need extra-whiskery perception to see things like that. *And* you need to have gone without breakfast as well!'

He moved closer to the ball, shielding the side nearest to Constable Knapweed with his paws. 'This distinguished-looking gentleman in blue,' he continued excitedly, 'seems to be chasing somebody. It looks to me very much like a deadly criminal for whom there is a large reward. They're running in and out of the bushes. Up hill and down dale . . .'

Dill's excitement was catching and Constable Knapweed could hardly contain himself as he took out his

notebook and began writing. 'Up hill . . . and . . . down . . . dale . . .' he repeated.

Dill sat back. 'Oh dear,' he said. 'What a shame.'

'What's up?' cried Constable Knapweed. 'What's gone wrong?'

'I'm afraid he's being held back by all the bones,' said Dill sadly. 'Hard luck.' He started to rise and then crouched down again. 'I say, that's a good idea!' he exclaimed. 'He's put them all down outside my kennel! I can't see exactly how many but there must be a good couple of dozen or so . . .'

'Couple . . . of . . . dozen . . . bones,' repeated Constable Knapweed as he began writing again.

'Or so . . .' added Dill. 'Now he's giving chase again.

'Oh, I can see it all. The crowds . . . the presentation of the medal for bravery . . . the sergeant's stripes . . .'

'Go on . . .' said Constable Knapweed excitedly. 'Go on. Don't stop there!'

Dill stood up and lifted the tent flap. 'I'm afraid it's fading,' he said. 'It's a bit difficult to concentrate on an empty stomach,' he added meaningly.

'Just you wait here,' said Constable Knapweed. 'I'll soon fix that. I shan't be long.'

Dill stared at the retreating figure in blue. 'I should have taken this up years ago,' he said. 'Next, please!'

The next person happened to be Mr Bayleaf and as he sat down Dill went into his routine again, closing his eyes and waving his paws mysteriously in the air before gazing into the crystal ball.

'I see this distinguished-looking gentleman with a beard,' he began at last. 'He's sitting in a deckchair sipping an iced drink while someone else digs the garden . . .'

'Arrh,' said Bayleaf. 'Now I like the sound of that. But who's digging the garden, that's what I'd like to know . . .'

Dill took a closer look at the crystal ball. 'I'm afraid I can't tell you that,' he said. 'There's a wheelbarrow full of bones in the way. I think the gentleman with the beard is about to take it as a present to the very deserving starving dog he knows . . .'

Bayleaf jumped to his feet. 'I shan't be long,' he called. 'I just 'as a call to make. Don't go away!'

'I shan't,' said Dill as he watched Mr Bayleaf go on his way. 'Just leave them with the others outside my kennel,' he called. 'Next, please!'

'This fish,' he announced as Sir Basil settled himself down, 'is so huge it's gone right off the ball. I can see neither head nor tail of it.'

Sir Basil took a firm grip of his fishing rod. 'Good gracious!' he exclaimed. 'Where's me net? I'll have it. I'll land the bounder.'

'I should be careful,' warned Dill as Sir Basil rose to his feet and made to leave. 'There's many a slip twixt pool and bank.' He lowered his voice confidingly. 'What you need is the help of a well-fed dog. The kind of dog who's dying to help because he's so full of energy-giving bones.'

'Bless me soul!' exclaimed Sir Basil. 'Where am I goin' to find one like that in the Herb Garden?'

Dill drew himself up to his full height. 'Find the bones

and leave them outside my kennel!' he announced in commanding tones. 'The hour will produce the dog!

'Between you and me, and the jolly old ball,' he added, gazing at his crystal ball as Sir Basil hurried off, 'I can see something else. I can see a dog enjoying his supper. Yums!'

*

It was late that evening when Parsley came across Dill. He was drawn towards his kennel by the sound of groans. Groans and moans and howls the like of which hadn't been heard in the Herb Garden for many a day.

'Oooooooooooooh!' groaned Dill as he drew near. 'Ooooooooooooow!'

'What's up?' asked Parsley, peering at him with interest.

'You're not *still* hungry,
are you? Shall I see if I
can find you another bone?'

'Ooooooowwwwwwww!' moaned Dill.
'Ooooooooooo!'

Parsley looked round. 'Don't say you've eaten them *all*?' he
exclaimed.

'Ooooooooooooh!' moaned Dill.

'The two dozen Constable Knapweed gave you?' asked Parsley.

'Or so,' groaned Dill.

'And the barrowload Mr Bayleaf left you.'

Dill nodded.

'And Sir Basil's?'

Dill nodded again.

'But there must have been dozens and dozens!' said Parsley.

'Forty-eight,' groaned Dill.

'I think I'd better have my ball back,' said Parsley.

'Take it!' groaned Dill. 'I never want to see it again.'

'I tell you what,' said Parsley. 'While I'm here
I'll tell you *your* fortune if you like.'

But Dill was having more than

enough trouble with his present to worry about the future.

'Poor old Dill,' said Parsley as he made his way back to his den. 'Fancy not wanting to have his fortune told. He must be in a bad way.

'On the other hand . . .' He thought for a moment. 'I don't really blame him.

'If I'd known gazing into a crystal ball would cause all this trouble I would have never taken it up in the first place. If you ask me there's no future in it.'

⁕Chapter 13

EXAM TIME

Mornings are usually the quietest time of the day in the Herb Garden. In fact, apart from the usual grunts and groans and snorts as one by one the various inhabitants come to life, not to mention an occasional sleepy hoot from Sage, the only sound to disturb the peace is that of Mr Onion's school bell summoning the Chives to their lessons.

Not that that bothers Parsley, because he doesn't have to go to school.

In a way, he rather likes hearing it, for the simple reason that he knows he can go back to sleep again as soon as it stops.

He said as much to himself one morning. 'Today,' he said, 'seems like a nice, quiet, restful day. As soon as Mr Onion stops ringing his bell I shall turn over and –' He gave an enormous yawn – 'do *nothing*!'

'Thank you,' he said as the bell stopped ringing.

He stretched himself out, closed his eyes and gave a deep sigh. 'I'm glad *I* don't have to go to school today,' he sighed dreamily. 'I don't feel at all scholastic today.'

The words were hardly out of Parsley's mouth before he heard a pounding of feet and he jumped up in alarm.

'It's either an earthquake,' he cried – for with his ear to the ground the pounding had sounded extra loud – '*or* it's a herd of elephants.'

But it turned out to be neither of those things.

A moment later all was revealed as a small figure came tearing round the corner and skidded to a halt beside him.

'I might have known,' said Parsley. 'Dill!'

He stepped back a pace in order to take in the sight, for it was no ordinary Dill who stood before him, tousled and unkempt after a night's sleep, but a highly polished and neatly brushed Dill. A Dill moreover who was wearing a cap and carrying a leather bag over one shoulder.

'Have you washed?' asked Parsley suspiciously.

Dill nodded frantically as he tried to get his breath back.

'Wonders will never cease!' exclaimed Parsley. He padded round Dill and examined him from the other side. 'And what's that thing you're carrying? It looks like a school satchel!'

Dill took an enormous deep breath. 'Haven't you heard?' he gasped. 'Haven't you heard? Mr Onion's holding his exams today and he's offering a prize to the one with the best answers. I've put both our names down for it!'

'You've *what*?' cried Parsley. He gave a groan. 'I knew it was too peaceful to last.'

Dill gave him a tug. 'Come on,' he cried. 'The bell's stopped ringing. We don't want to start off with a Late Slip. How many Ks in "scholar"? If I win we'll go shares if you like!'

Parsley gazed up at the sky as Dill dashed on ahead. 'Hark at him!' he exclaimed. 'If *he* wins. If he doesn't know how many Ks there are in "scholar" he won't stand a dog's chance!'

But all the same Parsley hurried after his friend and soon they were joining the throng of Chives making their way into the classroom.

They were only just in the nick of time for a moment later Mr Onion entered, carrying his stick and a large pile of papers.

As he mounted the platform the class stood to attention and awaited his word of command.

'Right,' he called. 'Chiiiives, sitting for exams, by numbers . . . begin.

'One, pause . . . two, pause . . . three.'

There was a clattering of seats and desk lids as the Chives, Parsley and Dill settled themselves down.

'Now, Chives,' continued Mr Onion as he paced up and down in front of the chalkboard, 'we are honoured today by the presence of Messrs Parsley and Dill.'

'Messrs?' repeated Dill out of the side of his mouth. 'I like that! You could eat bones off the floor of my kennel.'

'You often do,' agreed Parsley.

Mr Onion thumped the floor with his stick. 'Quiet in the ranks there!' he shouted.

'Shh!' whispered Parsley. 'We don't want to be kept in after school.'

'Messrs Parsley and Dill,' went on Mr Onion,

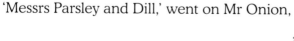

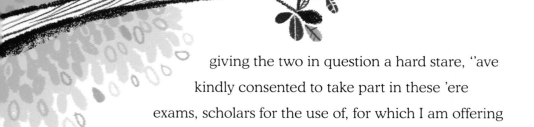

giving the two in question a hard stare, ''ave kindly consented to take part in these 'ere exams, scholars for the use of, for which I am offering a very valuable prize.'

Dill jumped to his feet. 'I think school is the finest thing there is, Mr Onion,' he called. 'May we have some sums, please?'

'Crawler!' hissed Parsley. 'Hard ones!' he added in a loud voice, not wishing to be outdone. 'The harder the better!'

'Hark who's talking now!' whispered Dill.

'Good lads!' said Mr Onion. 'That's what I like to 'ear. Stand up anyone who disagrees.'

There was a pounding of feet as all the Chives jumped up.

Mr Onion glared at them. 'You 'orrible lot!' he cried. 'Sit down at once. Just for that I shall start with a very difficult question indeed.' He turned to the board on which he'd already drawn a kind of rough circle with his chalk. 'Now, what do we 'ave 'ere?'

'A dirty chalkboard?' asked Dill, jumping to his feet again. 'I'll clean it for you if you like. Where's the duster?'

'A *dirty chalkboard*!' bellowed Mr Onion. 'I'll 'ave you know I

'ad to dig the potato what served as a model for this drawing afore you was up this morning. Anyone else?'

Parsley raised a paw. 'A beautifully drawn picture of an early potato?' he asked hopefully.

Mr Onion relaxed. 'Quite right,' he said. 'Good lad. I'm glad someone's paying attention. Now, if I was to take that potato off the board – which I can't on account of the fact that it's only drawn on – but if I did and I cut it in half, then I cut the two halves in half again, and then I cut those pieces in half, what would I 'ave?'

'Potato salad?' asked Dill hopefully.

Mr Onion gave Dill a dark glance. '*Potato salad!*' he snorted. 'Anyone else? Parsley?'

Parsley scratched his head. 'I . . . er . . . I ought to know,' he said, thinking hard. 'Er . . . potatoes . . . two from four is . . . er . . . carry one . . . um . . . It's a long time since I ate . . .'

'Eight is the correct answer!' barked Mr Onion. 'Good. That's one mark to Parsley.'

'Would you believe it?' murmured Dill. 'Of all the luck!'

'We will now turn to English Literature,

bards for the use of,' continued Mr Onion. 'That is,' he added, glaring at Dill, 'if certain dogs 'ave finished chattering. Now, if Shakespeare were alive today, what would he be famous for?'

'His age?' asked Dill.

'Wrong!' bellowed Mr Onion. 'Parsley?'

'Er . . . Shakespeare,' said Parsley. 'Er . . . I know the name . . . but it *would* be on the tip of my tongue if I had a big enough tongue . . . I'm just trying to place . . .'

'Correct!' barked Mr Onion. 'His *plays* of course. Another mark for Parsley, making two in all.'

'*Now* who's crawling?' asked Dill.

'Dogs who live in glass kennels shouldn't throw bones,' said Parsley primly.

'We come now,' bawled Mr Onion, 'to the subject of Natural 'Istory, birds and bees for the use of. Can anyone tell me what grows on *all* trees?'

Silence reigned in the classroom for a moment or two.

'Dill?' asked Mr Onion as Dill put up a paw to scratch his head.

'I don't know,' said Dill sadly.

'Bark!' said Mr Onion. 'Bark!'

'Wuff! Wuff!' said Dill excitedly.

Parsley shook his head. 'Wuff! Wuff!' he said. '*Really!*'

'Well, it could have been right,' replied Dill. 'There's many a true word spoken in wuffs.'

'There *are* other meanings to the word "bark",' said Parsley.

'Good!' called out Mr Onion. 'Bark is the correct answer.' He nodded approvingly. 'We've a good lad 'ere . . . That gives Parsley another mark and brings us to the end of the exams, pupils for the use of, making him the winner by a clear margin of three to nothing.'

'Congratulations!' said Dill, trying to make himself heard over the mountains of applause. 'I wonder when we get *our* prize? May I eat my share now?'

'*Our* prize?' repeated Parsley. 'You haven't answered a single question.'

'I did offer to go shares if *I* won it,' said Dill. 'Fair's fair.'

'The prize,' shouted Mr Onion, holding up his hand for quiet. 'The prize for the best exam result, which I now have pleasure in awarding to Parsley the lion, is a voucher, scholars for the use of, entitling the holder to a day off from school.'

Parsley stared at the piece of paper Mr Onion had given him. 'A day off from school?' he repeated as he read the words. 'But I don't even go to school!'

'You'd better start soon,' said Dill. 'Otherwise it won't be worth having. It's nearly the end of term.'

'Dogs!' said Parsley bitterly as they made their way home. '"Exams", "Go shares on the prize," he said!'

'We all have our wuff days,' panted Dill. 'Don't forget to be up early tomorrow . . . You've got a day off.'

'*We* have a half day off each,' said Parsley. '*We* are going shares, remember?'

Dill stood to one side. 'Bags you go first, then,' he said. 'I could do with a lie-in.'

'Bags I say goodnight,' said Parsley disgustedly. 'I'm going back to bed!'

✤Chapter 14

LOOKING FOR WORK

Like most lions, Parsley leads a fairly busy life. Although he enjoys a good lie-in in the mornings, when he does get up there's usually plenty to do. There is the weather to test, and trails to be followed before they have time to wear off – all manner of things, in fact.

On the other hand, like most lions and a good many people, even Parsley finds there are days when it's hard to think of something to do, and it so happened that when he woke the morning after the exams it was one of *those* days.

He came out of his den. Then he had a good stretch, sniffed the morning air, peered under a few bushes and . . . just sat.

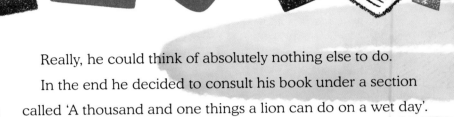

Really, he could think of absolutely nothing else to do.

In the end he decided to consult his book under a section called 'A thousand and one things a lion can do on a wet day'.

Although there wasn't a cloud in the sky he felt sure it would suggest something. And, sure enough, it did. It said: 'If you are a lion at a loose end, why not try advertising for work in the agony column of a newspaper?'

Parsley had never put any sort of advertisement in the agony column of a newspaper before, let alone one asking for work.

On the other hand, doing something is always better than doing nothing at all, so he sat down to write one out.

It took him a long time but at last it was ready and he sent it off post-haste to *The Herbs Review*, which as luck would have it was due out that very day.

Unlike most newspapers, which are made up of many sheets, *The Herbs Review* only brought out one page at a time.

It was published by Signor Solidago, the Italian music master, who used an old set with rubber type, and it took him so long to set up, by the time he'd finished one edition it was time to start on the next.

But luckily for Parsley there was still some room left at the bottom and so his advertisement arrived in time.

Quite a crowd gathered round Signor Solidago as he held the paper up for everyone to see. Aunt Mint, Constable Knapweed, Bayleaf, Dill – all jostled for a closer look.

'"Young lion at a loose end,"' read Aunt Mint. '"Requires . . . work!" Good gracious!'

Constable Knapweed peered over her shoulder. '"Go anywhere . . ."' he added.

'"Do anything . . ."' broke in Bayleaf.

'Fancy being able to advertise for *work*!' exclaimed Dill in amazement. 'What will they think of next? I mean . . . you can want *bones* or a good yawn . . . but *work*!' In order to prove his point Dill opened his mouth, gave a loud yawn, then closed his eyes and a moment later fell fast asleep.

'"Apply at path near gate for details,"' said Constable Knapweed.

He looked up from the paper. 'Where's my bucket? I'll soon find him a job of work to do.' And he hurried off to look for Parsley.

Constable Knapweed hadn't far to go for Parsley was as good as his word. He was waiting by the gate all agog for something to happen.

Constable Knapweed approached Parsley with his hands behind his back and circled him several times, apparently taking an unusual amount of interest in his tail.

'It occurs to me, young feller-me-lion,' he said at last, 'that a lad like yourself, with a fine tail and all, is wasted sitting around all day, squandering your time so to speak.'

Parsley put on a slightly superior expression. 'He's quite right, of course,' he said, addressing the empty air. He stood up and peered round at himself. 'I mean to say . . .' He waved his tail to and fro a couple of times. 'Just look at it . . .'

'Hanging there,' continued Constable Knapweed. 'Doing nothing, as you might say. It'd make a fine mop it would. A mobile mop!'

He took his hands from behind his back and placed a large galvanised bucket over Parsley's tail. 'You can dip it in this 'ere bucket,' he said triumphantly. 'And then go around mopping things up. There's always things what need mopping up in the Herb Garden. You won't be at a loss for something to do.'

Parsley stared after Constable Knapweed as he disappeared from view.

'My *tail*!' he exclaimed, hardly able to believe his ears. 'A *mop*! Hanging there . . . doing nothing, as you might say? *He* might say it! A mobile mop indeed! It's coming to something.'

But Parsley had hardly got over his feeling of indignation, let alone removed the bucket from his tail, when Mr Bayleaf appeared on the scene.

'Ah, there 'e be, Parsley,' he exclaimed. 'I 'ear you've turned over a new leaf.'

'Well,' said Parsley cautiously, 'I suppose you could put it that way if you like.'

'In that case,' said Bayleaf, 'I've been wondering if you'd like to turn over another one.'

'Would I like to . . .' Parsley stared at the bucket. 'Anything's better than this!'

'Good,' said Bayleaf, producing a broom from behind his back, ''cause I 'as plenty of leaves you can turn over. They b'ain't be new, but the garden's full of 'em.

'If I ties this 'ere broom on your tail . . . like so . . . you can turn 'em over as you go along. You'll 'ave a great pile of 'em in no time at all.'

While he was talking, Bayleaf busied himself tying the broom on to Parsley's tail with a piece of raffia.

'"As ye mops,"' he quoted, '"so ye shall sweep." Bayleaf, chapter seven, verse six. Tee! Hee! Hee!'

'Well!' exclaimed Parsley as Bayleaf went on his way, chuckling to himself. 'I'll be . . . Whatever next? Taking advantage of a lion, that's what it is. I've a good mind to . . .'

Parsley didn't really know what he had a good mind to do. Which was just as well, for at that moment Aunt Mint came into view.

'Ah, Parsley,' she called out. 'There you are. I've been looking for you everywhere. Now, don't move. Stay just as you are!'

Parsley froze in his tracks.

'I have a little surprise for you,' continued Aunt Mint. 'I read your advertisement in the paper and I know just the thing to pass the time.'

'At last!' said Parsley as Aunt Mint disappeared behind him. 'I knew if I waited long enough everything would turn out all right. It's about time too! Using my tail as a mop! Hanging buckets on it! Tying brooms to it!'

'You can look round now, Parsley,' called Aunt Mint.

Parsley gazed round hopefully at his tail and then nearly fell over backwards with surprise. Aunt Mint had tied a skein of wool to it! She'd also tucked several more into his mane.

'I knew you'd be surprised,' said Aunt Mint. 'Now, don't go away. I'm going to fetch some more wool. Then when I get back you can help me wind it into nice, round balls ready for my knitting. I've hundreds and hundreds to do. It'll keep you busy for weeks and weeks.'

'Would you believe it?' wailed Parsley as Aunt Mint hurried on her way. He raised his eyes to the heavens above. 'Would you believe it! All I wanted was something to pass the time!'

'Hullo!' called Dill as he raced on and began running round and round Parsley in circles. 'Going somewhere? You look as if you're all dressed up for something.'

'Grr,' said Parsley. 'It's all very well for you. You're not at a loose end.'

Dill skipped to a stop. 'Not at a loose end?' he repeated. '*Not at a loose end?*' He blinked several times in order to make sure he'd heard all right. 'Why, my end is so loose sometimes I can't even catch it.'

He ran round in circles a few more times. 'That's what I do when I'm at a loose end,' he panted. 'I run round and round in a circle and see where I end up.' He opened his eyes. 'Where are you?' he cried anxiously.

'I'm over here,' groaned Parsley.

Dill turned to face him. 'I do wish you'd stay still,' he complained. 'It's very confusing when you keep on moving about.' He took a closer look at Parsley. 'Do you know another thing I do?' he asked.

'No,' said Parsley. 'I'll buy it. What *do* you do?'

'I try lifting both my right legs off the ground,' said Dill.

'You mean – like this?' asked Parsley, doing his best to oblige.

Dill ran round to Parsley's right side in order to inspect him. 'That's right,' he said. 'Very good.

'Now,' he continued,

running round to the other side again. 'Try lifting both your left legs off the ground at the same time.'

'That,' he said sadly, when the noise of falling buckets and brooms had died down, 'is what always happens to me.'

'Ow!' cried Parsley, trying to disentangle himself from Aunt Mint's wool. 'Ohhhh! Ooooooooooooooh!' He glared at Dill. 'I shall never, never tell anyone I'm at a loose end again,' he wailed. 'And I shall never, never, ever advertise in an agony column.

'Ow!' He rubbed himself. 'I've often wondered how it got its name. Now I know!'

Chapter 15

PARSLEY'S TELEGRAM

One day Parsley was having a quiet after-lunch doze in the shade of one of the trees in the Herb Garden when he received a telegram – right on the end of his nose.

He opened his eyes and looked around, but there wasn't a soul in sight.

What a good job it wasn't a phone call, he thought, peering at the piece of paper. *That really would have hurt.*

He lay there for a moment or two trying to think who would possibly want to send him a telegram. Then, unable to bear the suspense a moment longer, he gave an extra-large yawn and got up in order to investigate the matter.

It was a very odd sort of telegram. In fact, the more he looked at it the stranger it seemed, for he couldn't make head or tail of it.

⅃HϽINOꞱ Ǝ∩ϽƎᗺꞸⱯᗺ Ɐ OꞱ, it said, ᗡƎꞱIⱯNI ƎᖯⱯ ∩O⅄.

In the end Parsley decided it could only mean one of two things. Either it was in a foreign language – like Russian or Chinese – or it was in some new and highly secret code.

But why anyone would want to send him a telegram in a foreign language he couldn't understand, or a code that was so secret he couldn't work it out, Parsley had no idea.

He decided to consult his friend Dill on the subject.

'I have this telegram,' he announced in a very superior tone of voice as he laid it down on the ground in front of Dill's kennel. 'I thought you might care to see it. It's a very rare sort of telegram. It's not only in a foreign language, it's probably in code as well!'

Dill, who was busy tucking into a pile of bones and really much too busy to worry about such trifling matters as telegrams, even if they were of a very rare kind, lay where he was, chewing for a while, before he even bothered to look up.

zzz zzz zᶻzᶻzᶻzᶻᶻ

'Foreign language?' he said at last, when he finally condescended to give it a passing glance.

Parsley nodded.

'Code?'

Parsley nodded again.

'You must have been looking at it upside down,' said Dill. 'It's from Aunt Mint.'

Dill began to feel very superior. He wasn't usually as good at reading as Parsley. 'I'll tell you what it says if you like,' he added carelessly.

Parsley gazed up at the sky with a bored 'you can if you like, but I'm not really bothered' expression on his face. 'Whatever takes your fancy,' he said. 'I was really only testing you.'

Dill cleared his throat of the remains of some bones. 'It's addressed to Parsley and Dill,' he began. 'Care of the Herb Garden. Then it goes on to say . . .'

Dill paused for a moment while he gave the piece of paper a closer inspection. Then he suddenly jumped to his feet, his eyes growing larger and larger, all thought of bones suddenly and unexpectedly driven from his mind.

'Good gracious!' he exclaimed. 'I don't believe it! It can't be true! She wouldn't want to, would she?'

He ran round and round in a circle several complete times before finally coming to rest beside the telegram again.

'She jolly well does!' he exclaimed, taking another look. 'It's all there in black and white!'

'What's all there?' asked Parsley impatiently. He looked at his friend with interest. Beneath its covering of fur, Dill's face seemed to have gone quite pale.

'Aunt Mint's going to cut our whiskers off!' exclaimed Dill. 'I must have another bone!' And without further ado he dived into the pile by his side and began chewing away as if his very life depended on it.

Parsley gave a chuckle. 'You won't believe this,' he said. 'But just for the moment I thought you said Aunt Mint wants to cut our whiskers off!'

'Uhhmmphhh!' said Dill, nodding his head violently between chews. 'Uhhhmmmphhhhhh! That's mppphhhhh what I mmmmphhhh did say!'

'*What?*' It was Parsley's turn to jump to his feet. 'Let me see it!' he cried. 'Where is it?'

Dill stopped chewing and looked around. 'I had it a moment ago,' he said. 'It was right here – alongside my pile of bones. Oh! . . . I . . . er . . . I . . . um . . . Oh!'

Parsley stared at him. 'Fancy *eating* a telegram!' he exclaimed in disgust. 'Now what are we going to do? We don't even know the when, the where or the how, let alone why!'

'*Do?*' said Dill, making a dive for the nearest bush. 'You must be joking. There's only one thing we can do. Go into hiding!'

And go into hiding they did. In a little-used part of the garden that was kept for special occasions – like sports days, bonfire nights and the odd occasions when dogs and lions wanted to go into hiding.

'Mind you,' said Parsley, after they had been there for a minute or two and the dust had settled down, 'I still can't understand it. I really can't understand Aunt Mint suggesting such a thing.'

He began prowling up and down while he turned the matter over in his mind. 'I mean to say, she's such a nice, kindly person. She wouldn't harm the hair on a dog's back let alone the whiskers on a lion's nose . . . It's not like her . . . It's not like her at all.'

He paused in mid-stride and looked around.

'You know,' he continued as he caught sight of Dill lying on his back with his paws in the air, 'one of the worst things about going into hiding is having to talk to yourself. I know just how Robinson Crusoe must have felt. What *are* you doing?'

'I'm saving myself,' said Dill simply. 'I'm letting all my energy run back into my brain in case I need it.'

Parsley snorted. 'That shouldn't take very long,' he said. 'Not with a brain your size.

'Are you sure you got it right? Are you absolutely, positively sure Aunt Mint said she wants to cut off our whiskers?'

Dill jumped to his feet. 'As sure as I'm lying here with my paws in the air,' he said.

'That,' said Parsley, 'is exactly what bothers me!'

Dill lay down again and closed his eyes. 'I can see it now. As plain as your face.'

'Thank *you*,' said Parsley. He gave a sniff. 'You know, changing the subject, I keep thinking I can smell something cooking.'

'It happens when you're hungry,' said Dill. 'That and sizzles. I keep thinking I can hear sizzles. I do wish I hadn't left my bones behind.'

'A whisker on the nose is worth two bones in the bush,' said Parsley firmly. 'You might not have any left if we'd waited.' His nose twitched again. 'You know, I *can* smell something cooking.'

Dill scrambled to his feet and joined Parsley in a long and appreciative sniff. 'It comes and goes,' he said. 'Sometimes it's there and sometimes it isn't.'

'Well,' said Parsley, 'I don't know about you, but *I'm* going to investigate it before it goes altogether.'

'Wait for me!' called Dill as Parsley disappeared up a nearby path. 'Don't leave me . . .'

Together they made their way deeper and deeper into the undergrowth. Several times Parsley stopped in order to make sure his sniffs were leading them in the right direction, but the further they went the stronger became the scent until even someone with hardly any sense of smell at all would have been hard put to make the wrong turning.

Neither of them knew quite what they would find at the end of the trail, but the very last thing they expected to stumble across was what looked like the remains of a party, and for a moment or two they stood staring at the sight open-mouthed.

SNIFF

SNIFF

SNIFF

There it all was; the smouldering remains of a camp fire, with a kind of open wire tray above it, and above that again – impaled on a long rod above the glowing embers, a plump, round, golden-brown object, dripping with sizzling fat.

'It's a mirage!' said Dill gloomily.

'It's a sausage!' exclaimed Parsley, taking a closer look. 'Someone's been holding a party.' As he looked around he caught sight of a pile of wool lying nearby. 'Aunt Mint's been holding a party. I'd recognise her knitting anywhere. She's been holding a barbecue.'

Parsley broke off. For some reason or other his words seemed to be having a strange effect on Dill, who was running around in circles as fast as he could go.

'That's it!' he cried. 'That's it! That's what she said in her telegram. Help! Save me! I knew it was right,' he panted. 'I knew

it! She said "you are both invited to a barber queue"!'

Parsley stared at his friend.

'A *barber* queue!' he repeated bitterly.

Dill skidded to a stop and nodded.

'How can anyone be so . . .' Parsley broke off, for once at a loss for words. 'She meant a *barbecue*!' he roared. 'That's an outdoor feast, with things grilled on a spit over an open fire. Oodles of hamburgers and sausages and . . . and . . . and we've missed it!'

'Oh well,' said Dill sadly. 'We all make mistakes. Anyway, I never did like sausages very much. They never have any bones in them.'

Parsley took a step nearer. 'That,' he said menacingly, 'can be fixed. Come here!'

Parsley's roar of disgust was drowned by Dill's howl of alarm as he disappeared in the direction of the kennel.

'Barbecue,' said Parsley, examining the by now charred remains of the sausage. '*Barber* queue! That's the last time I let anyone else read *my* telegrams!'

Chapter 16

DILL'S STATELY KENNEL

One day Parsley was browsing through his copy of *What's On in the Herb Garden* when he came across an entry marked DILL DAY.

It must be pretty important, he thought. *They don't put three lots of crossed bones by the side of these things for nothing. I'd better go and see what's what as well as what's on!*

So he set off down one of the many garden paths that led to Dill's kennel.

Like most lions, Parsley was very good at following trails, and in any case he knew the Herb Garden like the back of his paw, so he could really have done the journey with his eyes closed if he'd wanted to. He was all the more surprised, therefore, to discover that on practically every tree he came across someone had nailed a blue arrow to point the way.

In fact, the whole thing was so unusual he spent more time looking at the arrows than he did watching where he was going, and because the arrows were fixed very close to the ground he was taken even more by surprise than he might have been when he rounded a corner and walked slap bang into a table, behind which sat Dill himself.

'What on earth's going on?' asked Parsley when he had recovered from the shock. 'I was just on my way to see you.'

Dill held up a paw to bar the way. 'Have you booked?' he asked.

'*Booked?*' repeated Parsley. 'What do you mean . . . booked?'

'I'm throwing my kennel open for the day,' said Dill carelessly. He nodded towards a sign standing beside an open box on the table. 'I'm afraid it's ticket holders only this way. If you want to pay at the door you'll have to follow the red arrows and take your turn.'

Parsley stared at his friend in amazement. 'A *ticket?*' he exclaimed. '*Follow the red arrows?* Have I ever asked you for a ticket when you've been to see me?'

Dill coughed and pretended to examine the end of one of his paws. 'Well,' he said, giving a slightly superior laugh, 'that *is* a little different, isn't it? I mean . . . I don't like to say it, but . . . er . . . who'd want to buy a ticket just to see your den? My kennel's been handed down.'

'From where I'm standing it looks more as if it's been thrown down,' exclaimed Parsley sarcastically. He peered past the table at the wooden building beyond. 'Don't tell me people are actually falling for this diabolical scheme.'

'Take a look for yourself,' said Dill, bowing low as two familiar figures strolled past. 'Good morning, Sir Basil. Good morning, Lady Rosemary.

'You may like to see the family motto,' he called after them. 'It's just inside over the front door. You can't miss it. "Pro Bono", it says—'

'Don't you mean "*Pro Bono Publico*"?' broke in Parsley as Sir Basil and Lady Rosemary disappeared through the door of the kennel. 'It's Latin. It means "For the Public Good".'

'I know what I mean,' said Dill firmly. 'Catch me giving away all my bones to the public.'

He lowered himself to the ground again as two more figures came into view. 'Good morning, Constable Knapweed. Good morning, Mr Bayleaf. I'm *so* glad you could come.'

Parsley looked down at his friend in disgust. 'If you bow any lower,' he exclaimed, 'you won't have any fur left on your chin. It's disgusting.'

'Make yourselves at home,' called Dill, choosing to ignore the remark. 'And don't forget to look at my bed.'

'Look at your *bed*?' repeated Parsley. 'What's so special about your bed?'

'Fido the third once slept there,' said Dill impressively. 'You can still see the marks on the wood where he gnawed in his sleep.'

'Talking of visitors,' said Parsley. 'I have a feeling you're about to acquire another one.' He pointed back down the path to where a very large metal object had just come into view. '*That* could only be Pashana Bedhi!'

'Good morning, Parsley. Good morning, Dill.' Pashana Bedhi, the chef, paused to mop his brow as he drew level. 'My goodness me! If only I'd left my chef's pot at home . . . that is what I keep telling myself. If only I'd left my chef's pot at home.'

'He won't be the only one saying that when he gets inside your kennel,' murmured Parsley as Mr Bedhi went on his way. 'I should think that's all they need in there – a chef with his own chef's pot.'

'You're *sure* you wouldn't like a ticket?' asked Dill. 'I could stretch a point in your case and let you use the blue entrance. *And* I'm throwing in a free tea at the end of the tour into the bargain.'

Parsley shuddered. 'No, thank you,' he said. 'I've had some of your free teas before. Half a bowl of bone soup and a slice of rock cake. And when I said I'd like another slice you told me to break the first one in two!'

'Shh!' said Dill as the sound of marching feet reached their ears. 'I think I may have some more customers.'

As he spoke a cloud of dust rose above some nearby bushes and a moment later the Chives swung into view with Mr Onion at their head.

'Chives . . . Chiiiives, halt!' Mr Onion's voice rang out. 'Chives . . . stand at ease. Stand eeeasy!'

Having brought his class safely to a halt outside the kennel, Mr Onion gave Dill a smart salute and then began pacing up and down in order to deliver a lecture.

'Now, Chives,' he announced. 'You are about to go on your annual school treat, pupils for the benefit of. I want you to enjoy yourselves at all times and to behave as if you were in your own home. No drawing on the walls or throwing pellets, ink; otherwise there will be no more annual outings this year. Is that understood?'

Having received a chorus of agreement from his class, Mr Onion brought them to attention again.

'Right, Chives,' he bellowed. 'Visiting Dill's kennel, by numbers . . . begin. Hep . . . two, three, four. Hep . . . two, three, four.'

'I say,' exclaimed Parsley as one by one the long line of Chives disappeared from view, 'you're packing them in a bit, aren't you?'

'Can I help it if it's popular?' asked Dill. 'I have to cater for the tour groups as well, you know.'

'Steady on there!' bellowed Mr Onion as he followed the last of the Chives in through the kennel door. 'We don't want to go waking all the ancestors, Dill's family for the use of.'

'Ancestors?' exclaimed Parsley. 'What ancestors?'

'I didn't just happen, you know,' replied Dill stiffly. 'We Dills have been in the Herb Garden from time unimaginable. Why, some of my ancestors are so ancestral they wouldn't even speak to you if they were alive today!'

'That,' said Parsley, 'bothers me not a lot. In fact, I don't even give a hoot. But here comes someone who would.'

Sage, the owl, stared at the others suspiciously as he hopped into view. 'Tu whit, tu whoo,' he hooted. 'Which is the tu whit, tu way in?'

Parsley gave Dill a nudge. 'He'll never make it,' he hissed. 'There's sixteen inside already. Even without feathers he'd never make it.'

Dill began to look worried. 'You could be right,' he admitted grudgingly. 'You could be right about that.'

'I'm sorry,' he called. 'We're full up at the moment. If you'd care to wait . . .'

Sage glared back over his shoulder. 'Full up?' he hooted. 'Tu whit, tu wait? I bought my ticket tu whit, tu days ago! I'm going in . . .' And without further ado he began banging loudly on the front door with his beak. 'Let me in!' he hooted. 'Let me in!'

''Ere, steady on!' Constable Knapweed's voice rose above the din as the door burst open and Sage tried to force his way in. 'Stop that there shoving. Stand back, everyone. Otherwise there'll be a nasty accident and I won't be 'eld responsible for the consequences.'

But the words had hardly left Constable Knapweed's mouth before the worst began to happen.

There was a loud creaking noise, and Dill's kennel, which had been swaying gently to and fro for the last few minutes, gradually began to move from its spot – rather as if it had been gripped by some large, yet invisible hand.

'I don't want to worry you,' said Parsley, 'but I hope you've got some change-of-address cards printed. I think you're about to move house any moment now.'

Dill stood rooted to the spot as he gazed at the sight. 'But I don't want to move house!' he wailed. 'I've always lived there.'

'Perhaps you'll find somewhere with a good view,' said Parsley comfortingly as the kennel glided past, propelled by the weight of all its occupants.

Dill began running round and round in circles. 'It's all very well for you,' he cried, 'but it's no joke seeing your home disappear before your very eyes without so much as a by-your-leave.'

'If you run you may catch it,' said Parsley. 'There probably won't be another one going past for hours. You could nip through the back door and put a stop to things before it's too late.'

Dill came to a halt. 'What back door?' he said gloomily. 'You know very well I haven't got one.'

'I think you have now,' said Parsley as a loud crash echoed round the clearing.

He gave a sigh as the kennel rebounded from tree to tree and a series of bangs and crashes rent the air.

'There goes one of the

Stately Kennels of England. It's rather sad, really, the way they're disappearing one by one. Still, you did want to open it to the public.' He put a paw to his ear. 'It sounds as if it's getting more and more open every moment.'

Dill turned to the table and picked up the tray. 'Would you care to make a small donation?' he asked hopefully. 'It's for a very good cause. The Dill Kennel Restoration Fund.'

Parsley shook his head. 'No, thank you! I've a much better idea.'

'This way for Parsley's Den,' he called as he hurried up the path after the others. 'Get your tickets here. Open to the public for one day only. No connection with the firm that *was* next door. This way for Parsley's Den. Get your tickets here . . .'

Chapter 17

DILL'S RESTAURANT

D ill was very busy for the next few days, and the Herb Garden resounded with the noise of sawing and hammering and banging as he put his kennel to rights.

Having no wish to get boarded in, or knocked over by a plank, or have his paws squashed by a hammer, Parsley stayed well clear and so he wasn't really prepared for the sight that met his eyes when he did eventually pay a call on his friend.

Since he'd last seen it Dill's kennel had undergone something of a transformation. In fact, it didn't look like an ordinary common-or-garden kennel any more.

Outside the front door were several tables and chairs – each with its own sunshade. To one side there was a loudspeaker out of which came some French accordion music, and around the door were rows and rows of badges.

Even Dill himself had changed, for he was wearing a white chef's hat and a tunic, and he was bustling to and fro with a notepad and pencil in a very important manner.

'What on earth's going on?' asked Parsley.

'Don't stop me,' panted Dill. 'I'm much too busy. I'm going round and round in circles this morning.'

'I can see that,' said Parsley. 'But what's going on?'

Dill paused for a moment. 'I'm opening a restaurant,' he announced, waving a paw at the tables. 'I'm waiting for the inspector now.'

'The *inspector*?' repeated Parsley.

'The Good Bone Inspector,' explained Dill impatiently. 'I shouldn't be surprised if he doesn't award me a crossed bone or two in the Guide.'

Parsley licked his lips. 'Can anyone eat here?' he asked.

Dill looked at him doubtfully. 'I suppose so,' he said. 'I have to be a bit careful, you know. I don't want to lower the tone of the place.'

Parsley stared at him. 'You don't want to lower the tone of the place?' he repeated. 'This is me . . . Parsley . . . your friend!'

'I might be able to squeeze you in,' said Dill reluctantly. He led the way to one of the tables. 'You're really supposed to have a reservation, of course . . .'

'Thank you very much,' said Parsley sarcastically as he sat down. 'It's nice of you to go to so much trouble.'

'It's all part of the service,' said Dill. 'What would you like to eat?'

Parsley picked up the menu and studied it for a moment. 'I think I'll start with some asparagus soup,' he announced. 'Then I'll have lobster mayonnaise, and a double ice cream to follow.'

'I'm afraid they're off,' said Dill promptly.

'All of them?' exclaimed Parsley. 'It's a bit soon, isn't it? You've only just opened. What *have* you got?'

'There's some very good bone soup,' said Dill. 'I can recommend that. It's still a bit hot. I've just put my tongue in to test it. But you get a reduction if you lick the bowl clean before one o'clock.'

'I don't like bone soup,' said Parsley.

Dill thought for a moment. 'Well, there's bones and chips,' he said. 'Bones and peas . . . bones and custard . . .'

'Haven't you got anything other than bones?' asked Parsley. 'I shouldn't like to take my custom elsewhere,' he added meaningly. 'After all, I might bump into the inspector!'

'I have got a steak,' said Dill reluctantly. 'I was really saving it till later. I . . .' He caught sight of the look on Parsley's face. 'I'll go and light the oven,' he said hastily.

'I should think so too!' exclaimed Parsley as Dill disappeared into his kennel, and he settled down to wait.

But a moment later Dill was back. 'Have you got a match?' he asked.

Parsley started at him. 'I have so many matches on me,' he said, 'I'm frightened to bend over quickly in case I blow up. Lions don't have matches!'

'Neither do dogs,' said Dill. 'But I'm having a bit of a problem with the stove at the moment—'

'Policemen have matches,' broke in Parsley. 'They have everything.' He nodded towards a figure making its way along the garden path. 'Ask Constable Knapweed. He's just coming.'

'Hullo, hullo,' said Constable Knapweed as he drew near. 'What's going on here?' He withdrew his notebook and surveyed the scene. 'A restaurant? In the Herb Garden? I hope you've got permission for this, young Dill?' He gave a sniff. 'We don't want to 'ave the smell of cooking everywhere.'

'There's not much fear of that,' murmured Parsley. 'Not the way things are going.'

'I was only going to serve snacks,' said Dill hastily. 'Like cups of tea to policemen when they're thirsty on a hot day. And steaks . . .'

Constable Knapweed looked up. 'Oh,' he said. 'Oh, well. Mmmm, that's different. No one can say I'm a hard man. Did I hear the word "tea" mentioned?'

'And steaks,' said Dill eagerly.

Constable Knapweed snapped his notebook shut. 'I'll 'ave a table near the loudspeaker,' he said. 'I like a bit of music when I'm enjoying a good meal.'

'The thing is,' broke in Parsley, 'the chef needs a match – to light the stove.'

'A match?' Constable Knapweed felt in his pocket and withdrew a box. 'Why ever didn't you say so before?' He crossed to the kennel door. 'Why, I'll have that stove alight and the kettle on the boil before you can say one lump or two.'

'Oh dear,' said Dill as Constable Knapweed disappeared from view.

'What's the matter, *garçon*?' asked Parsley.

'I forgot to turn the gas off,' said Dill.

Parsley stared at him. 'You mean it's been turned on all the time we've been talking?' he asked.

'Full on,' said Dill. 'It's been going for ages now.'

The words were hardly out of his mouth before a violent explosion shook the ground.

'It sounds as though it's gone altogether now,' said Parsley as they picked themselves up. 'And bang goes our steak as well!'

Constable Knapweed, his helmet askew, peered out through the open door. 'Matches!' he exclaimed bitterly.

'I've got a picture of a steak,' said Dill as they hid behind one of the tables. 'In colour!'

'A *picture* of one?' repeated Parsley. 'What's the good of that? You can't eat a picture.'

'You can if you're really hungry,' said Dill. 'I've often done it. There's some custard left over from yesterday and it won't be too bad if you close your eyes. How about it?'

'Bring me some scissors,' said Parsley wearily. 'We'll go shares if you like.'

Chapter 18

DILL'S POP GROUP

One day, soon after the episode with Dill's restaurant, Parsley was out for a walk in the Herb Garden when he heard a strange pinging sound.

'*Ping! Ping! Ping!*'

'It's either a woodpecker with a cracked beak,' he decided, 'or someone's left a tap dripping into a bucket.'

But as it turned out it was neither of these things. It was Dill. He was running round and round in circles calling out '*Ping*' to himself.

'*Ping! Ping! Ping!*' he said as Parsley drew near, '*Ping, diddy, ping, ping . . . ping, ping!*'

PING!
PING!
PING!

'Good gracious!' said Parsley. 'What on earth
are you up to now?'

'Just tuning up,' said Dill. '*Ping! Ping! Ping!*'

'Tuning up?' repeated Parsley. 'I say, you *are* all right? You
haven't been sitting out in the sun too much?'

Dill looked up at the cloud-filled sky. 'You must be joking,' he
said. '*Ping! Ping! Ping!*'

'Well, whatever sends you,' said Parsley. 'But there must be
something. People don't go around saying "*Ping! Ping! Ping!*" for
nothing.'

'Pop groups do,' said Dill. 'They do it all the time. *Ping! Ping! Ping!*'

'Pop groups?' repeated Parsley.

'I've given up being a restauranteur,' said Dill carelessly. 'I'm
taking up the guitar instead. Only I haven't got one and it's a bit
difficult with paws anyway, so I go "*Ping! Ping! Ping!*" instead.'

'Can anyone join in?' asked Parsley.

Dill thought for a moment. 'What can you play?' he asked
cautiously. 'I may have a waiting list.'

'What can I play?' said Parsley. '*What can I play?*'

'Well?' said Dill.

'There's the drums,' said Parsley. '*Boom! Boom!*'

'Do you think it'll catch on?' asked Dill. 'I mean, will *they* like it? The fans?'

'If you can get away with *ping! ping! ping!*,' said Parsley, 'I'm sure they'll like my *booms*.'

'All right,' said Dill. 'You're in. Only don't expect too many solo passages to start with. The guitar's getting most of those.'

'How about forming a group?' said Parsley excitedly. 'A quintet . . . we can hold auditions . . .'

'Do you think we'll find ten others?' asked Dill gloomily.

'*Ten* others?' exclaimed Parsley. 'It's a good job I came along. You'd have ended up with a brass band before you could say "The Herb Garden's Got Talent".'

He thought for a moment. 'Now, what we need is a name.'

'I did wonder about "The Herbs",' said Dill.

'Great! Marvellous!' said Parsley. He took up a stance and lowered his voice. 'The Herbs! Open for engagements . . . tea parties . . . soirees . . . elevenses . . .'

He began pacing up and down. 'I can see it all. We'll be famous . . . our name in lights . . . Golden discs . . .'

'Would you like my autograph now?' broke in Dill excitedly. 'I may be a bit tied up later.'

'Just put it at the bottom of my contract,' said Parsley. 'Let's go . . . the sooner we start the auditions the sooner we can retire.'

Parsley wasn't the only one to be excited at the thought of joining Dill's group. It seemed as though everyone in the Herb Garden wanted to take part. The notice had only been up a moment or so before they had a long list of applicants waiting to be auditioned.

'Right,' said Parsley. 'Who's first?'

Dill consulted his list. 'Sage,' he announced. 'Whistles and chirps a speciality.'

'That's not a very good start,' said Parsley as Sage hopped into view. 'Still, I suppose we'd better see him now he's here. We shall never hear the last of it otherwise.'

'Right,' he called. 'It's all yours. Take it away.'

'Tu whit, tu whoo,' said Sage.

The others waited a moment or two and when nothing else happened they began to get a bit restive.

'Tu whit, tu whoo?' said Parsley. 'Is that all? I can't see us getting to the top of the charts with that.'

'Don't call us,' said Dill, crossing Sage's name from his list. 'We'll call you.'

'Grrrrrrmph!' hooted Sage grumpily as he hopped away.

'Perhaps we could form a quartet,' said Parsley. 'Big bands are out anyway. Who's next?'

'Mr Bayleaf,' said Dill. 'With "Songs my mother taught me".'

'I don't want to worry you,' said Parsley out of the side of his mouth as Bayleaf entered, carrying a large pile of music, 'but it looks as though his mother had a large repertoire. I can see us ending up with a trio. It's not exactly the cream of the light-entertainment world.'

'Arrrh!' said Bayleaf. 'If you be ready.'

'Ready,' said Parsley resignedly. 'A one, a two, a three.'

Bayleaf drew a deep breath and broke into his song.

> *'I'm Bayleaf, I'm the gardener,*
> *I work from early dawn.*
> *You'll find me sweeping the leaves*
> *And tidying the lawn . . .'*

He looked up from his music. 'Arrh!' he exclaimed. ''Tis a real old 'un that. They don't write songs like that any more.'

'I'm not surprised,' said Parsley.

'Did they ever?' asked Dill.

'Next verse coming up,' said Bayleaf, ignoring the remarks.

'You mean . . . there's *more?*' exclaimed Parsley.

Bayleaf cleared his throat. 'There be forty-two all told,' he said, and before the others could stop him he was into the next verse.

> *'I'm Bayleaf, I'm the gardener,*
> *You'll see me sowing seeds,*
> *You'll find me lighting bonfires,*
> *And pulling up the weeds. Arrrh!'*

'Thank you very much,' said Parsley hastily as he ushered Mr Bayleaf on his way. 'We'll let you know later.'

'*Much* later!' agreed Dill.

'You don't appreciate good music, you don't,' growled Bayleaf. 'That be the trouble with you young 'uns. You're all the same . . . don't appreciate good music.'

'Who's next?' said Parsley as Bayleaf's voice died away. 'Whoever it is it couldn't be worse.'

'Do you want to bet?' asked Dill.

'It's Constable Knapweed! "Leaves from my notebook". A song, a dance and a whistle or two?' groaned Parsley. 'We all know what *that's* going to be like!'

'Well, young feller-me-lion,' said Constable Knapweed. 'And what *is* it going to be like?'

Parsley jumped as he felt the constable's hand on his shoulder. 'Very good, I should think, Constable Knapweed,' he said hastily. 'First class . . . er . . . if you like that sort of thing.'

'Hmm,' said Constable Knapweed sternly. 'I'm pleased to 'ear you say that. I wouldn't want to 'ave to take you into custody for unseemly behaviour while I'm in the middle of my act.'

He cleared his throat.

'Me, me, me me . . .

'Bumblebee, bumblebee,
Wonderful thing,
Of you and you only,
I ever will sing.
Bumblebee, bumblebee,
So small and sweet.
I relish your honey –
My favourite treat!'

As Constable Knapweed launched into his song Parsley led Dill to one side.

'This could go on for hours,' he said, 'and probably will.'

'I bet the Beatles didn't have all this trouble getting started,' said Dill.

Parsley gave a sigh. 'Oh, I don't know,' he said. 'Who wants to be a Beatle? You've only got to fall over on your back once and you're finished. You never get up again.'

'I suppose we could form a duet,' said Dill. 'We shan't need so many bulbs when we have our name in lights.'

'Either that,' said Parsley, 'or we can retire now while we're still at our peak. How about it?'

'I'll give you a ping,' said Dill. 'Don't wait up.'

'Don't worry,' said Parsley. 'I shan't. Goodnight!'

THE END